"Just who do you think you are?"

"I thought we'd established that. I'm your husband."

"In name only." Leigh lashed back.

"I'm quite prepared to rectify that if you'd care to oblige...?" Raoul's eyes were mocking. "I seem to remember that we were good together once."

"Are you sure it was us you are thinking of? There have been so many women in your life, Raoul, I'm surprised you can remember any one liaison."

Dear Reader,

HELEN BROOKS is an author with a growing reputation. Her books are emotional, involving, and bursting with romantic intensity! She is particularly talented at capturing the depth of feeling between a married couple...so we know you'll enjoy in *A Heartless Marriage*.

The Editor

Books by Helen Brooks

HARLEQUIN ROMANCE
3350—AND THE BRIDE WORE BLACK
3378—ANGELS DO HAVE WINGS

Look out for Helen Brooks's next title at Harlequin Reader Service: *Fire Beneath the Ice* appears in May 1997.

HELEN BROOKS

A Heartless Marriage

Harlequin Books

TORONTO • NEW YORK • LONDON
AMSTERDAM • PARIS • SYDNEY • HAMBURG
STOCKHOLM • ATHENS • TOKYO • MILAN
MADRID • WARSAW • BUDAPEST • AUCKLAND

ISBN 0-373-11844-9

A HEARTLESS MARRIAGE

First North American Publication 1996.

Copyright © 1993 by Helen Brooks.

This edition published by arrangement with Harlequin Books S.A.

® and TM are trademarks of the publisher. Trademarks indicated with
® are registered in the United States Patent and Trademark Office, the
Canadian Trade Marks Office and in other countries.

Printed in U.S.A.

CHAPTER ONE

'IT'S been a long time, Leigh.'

As the deeply caressing, velvet-smooth voice with its faint tinge of a French accent spoke just behind her Leigh's blood froze. She had known this would happen one day but had been unable to prepare herself for it, in the same way that she couldn't control the snaking shiver that crept down her spine as the unmistakable voice touched a spot deep inside her.

'Hello, Raoul.' She turned slowly as her mind raced, without attempting to smile, to meet the full force of that piercing ice-blue gaze that had once had the power to take her to heaven or hell. 'Five years, in fact.'

'And two months?' He looked devastatingly handsome, more so, if possible, than the last time she had seen him. He was just the same and yet...different. The intervening time-span had carved a few lines around his eyes and mouth but they merely added to the tanned perfection of a face that was stunningly beautiful in its complete maleness.

The strong straight nose, aristocratic chin and warm, sensual mouth would have been a master-piece if captured in oils, and the wild shock of thick black curly hair that she recalled had been groomed into a more sedate style that added extra emphasis to the darkly lashed, wicked blue eyes.

'You see, I remember.' He, too, was making no attempt to smile or lighten the situation, and a sudden little dart of resentful anger at his cool self-possession turned the soft brown of her eyes slate-hard. He was just the same after all! Just as arrogantly cold, just as casually cruel, just as——

'You are well?' Now the dazzling white teeth flashed in acknowledgement of her nod. 'That is good.'

'And you?' This was ridiculous, she thought helplessly, to stand and talk in polite clichés as though they were distant acquaintances renewing some tenuous connection, when really——

'I too am well.' The vivid blue eyes wandered lazily over her flushed face, lingering for a moment on the tremulous, soft mouth before travelling to the rich dark brown hair that hung down below her shoulders. 'You have grown your hair. I like it this way.' The touch of hauteur caused her chin to rise a fraction.

'Thank you.' I shall scream in a minute, Leigh thought desperately as she felt the blood begin to sing in her ears. She hadn't felt so exposed, so vulnerable, in years. Five years, in fact. She knew her hands were clamped together as though in a vice, the knuckles white with tension, but she couldn't have unwound them to save her life. She steeled herself to meet those piercing eyes again and forced a polite smile to her lips. 'Are you in England on business?' she asked coolly.

'In a way,' he smiled easily, obviously totally unaffected by her presence anyway, Leigh thought
bitterly. 'I suppose you could call it that.'

'Oh...' She couldn't think of another thing to
say; her mind had suddenly gone blank. 'Well...'
She glanced round helplessly as she took a small
step backwards. 'I'd better be——'

'I hear you are doing very well at your painting
now, Leigh.' As her eyes snapped back up to his
she searched his face for mockery and found none.
Instead she found interest, and something else...
Something that made her breath catch in her throat
and her head swim. He had no right to look at her
like that! No right at all. 'You are just as beautiful
as I remember.' His voice was husky and for a
moment the memories flooded in in vivid pain-
fulness. How many times had she woken from a
night spent in his arms to hear him say she was
beautiful? That she was his treasure? That he would
never let her go?

'I've never been beautiful, Raoul,' she said coldly
as she forced the hurt from her voice.

'You have, to me, always.' She really couldn't
take much more, she thought wildly. She had
looked forward to this occasion for weeks, knowing
that there would be many prestigious artists among
the throng of idle rich that always attended Nigel
Blake's little 'gatherings' as he liked to call them.
Nigel prided himself on getting just the right
mixture of up and coming artists and wealthy in-
fluential titles to make his parties the talk of
London. There had been more than one struggling

artist who had been set on the road to fabulous wealth by a commission at one of Nigel's 'do's.

'I need to talk to you, Leigh.' As Raoul placed his hand on her arm she actually jolted with the shock of it. An electric current more dangerous than anything harnessed by man shot through her body and she took a step backwards, her eyes enormous.

'I'm sorry, Raoul,' she said quickly, appalled he could still affect her so violently, 'but I don't want to talk to you.'

'Now that isn't kind.' Was that some kind of dark amusement she saw in those ice-blue eyes? 'I've been a patient man, Leigh, but there are still matters we need to discuss. Surely you can understand that?'

'What do you mean?' She stared at him, mesmerised by his audacity.

'Oh, come, come.' The accent was more pronounced now and those magnetic eyes drew her into him just as they had always done. 'You didn't think we would always remain in some sort of timeless limbo? You surely knew there would be a day of reckoning?' He smiled with slow cruelty.

'Well, Leigh, honey...' As the harsh American female voice sounded in her ear Leigh breathed a sigh of relief. She had never expected in her wildest dreams that she would ever be pleased to see Vivien James but just at this precise moment the tall willowy blonde was an answer to prayer. 'It's not fair to monopolise all the talent!' Leigh had heard the outrageous come-on before but Vivien always counted on the fact that the man in question hadn't, and now she glided seductively close.

'I'm Vivien.' The six-foot model stuck out a slender hand for Raoul to shake as she wriggled an invitation no man could ignore.

'Of course you are.' Raoul was a few inches taller than the beautiful blonde, his long lean body and big broad shoulders giving an impression of even greater height, and Leigh noticed, with a stab of apprehension, that his handshake was cursory and his smile tight. She knew the signs. He suffered fools badly.

'Well, I do suspect Leigh has been holding out on us,' Vivien gushed prettily. 'They say the quiet ones are the worse, don't they?' She laughed throatily, totally sure of herself and of the beauty that had taken her monthly salary into six figures in the last two years. 'Don't tell me you're an old friend?' She pouted provocatively as she touched Raoul's arm.

'I wouldn't dream of it,' Raoul said quietly, his eyes cold.

'No?' Vivien's predatory eyes gleamed, dismissing Leigh's presence with regal indifference as she edged forward, almost elbowing the other woman out of the way. 'What, then?'

'Leigh's husband, as it happens.' There was a positively diabolical glint of satisfaction in those cold blue eyes as they noted the stunned surprise on the carefully made-up face, the mouth an O of bewilderment.

'You're joking.' Vivien stared at Raoul, her eyes flicking over the tall lean body and film-star good looks before moving on to Leigh's medium height, slightly plump frame which housed a pretty but totally unpretentious face, the straight brown hair and large brown eyes ordinary by anyone's standards. 'I don't believe you. You can't be married to *her*!'

Her meaning was clear and as Leigh flushed painfully Raoul's face darkened. When he next spoke his voice was cutting, the accent as sharp as glass. 'Then that is your problem, yes?' He had taken Leigh's arm as he spoke, his attitude both protective and proprietorial, moving her away from the other woman into a quiet corner of the crowded room.

'Let go of me.' As she shook off his hand the urge to lash out was paramount, but she took a long, deep breath before facing him again, the anger that was coursing through her body giving her the courage to look deep into the piercing eyes without flinching. 'Why did you tell her that? And why are you here? I don't want you in my life.'

'I'm aware of that.' He was standing quite still now, the total lack of movement disquieting. 'Nevertheless, it is the truth. You are my wife, Leigh.' Her skin prickled helplessly as he turned her to face him with her back to the room so that her face was shielded from curious eyes. 'And don't look like that. I'm not going to hurt you.'

'You aren't going to...?' Her voice trailed away in a tight bitter laugh that turned his face into stone.

'What could you do to me that you haven't already done, Raoul? I loathe you, I detest you. If you were halfway decent you would have given me a divorce as soon as I left you.'

'I didn't want to.' His arrogance made her blink. 'Why didn't you file for one later?'

'Why?' She stared at him. 'You really want to know? Because I wanted to shut even the slightest thought of you out of my mind. I wanted to pretend that you didn't exist, that our marriage had never happened.' It wasn't the whole truth. A divorce had been almost unimportant compared to the excruciating step she had taken in leaving him in the first place. She had known she would never marry again. He was too hard an act to follow. 'I expected you to contact me anyway.' She raised her chin slightly. 'Is that why you are here now? To ask for a divorce? This meeting isn't by accident, is it?'

'No, it is not.' His eyes were slicing into her.

'What's her name?' she asked coldly. 'Surely Marion isn't still around?' She forced herself to say the hated name.

'I don't intend to discuss our private affairs here,' Raoul said tightly, 'but suffice it to say I am not here to ask for a divorce. How soon can you leave?'

'How soon can I . . . ?' For the second time in as many minutes she was speechless. 'You don't seriously think I'm going anywhere with you, do you? For all you know, I'm with someone.' She waved distractedly at the crowded room.

'Are you?' The glittering eyes challenged her, his mouth twisting in a faint smile as she tossed her head without replying. 'I thought not. Jeff Capstone is in Scotland, isn't he?' It was a cool statement of fact and delivered with icy disdain. 'You see, I know more about you than you think.' His eyes never left her face for an instant.

She stared at him in amazement as seething resentment turned her brown eyes black. 'How dare you?' Her voice, though low, was full of scathing contempt. 'Just who do you think you are?' She couldn't believe the pretentious insolence.

'I thought we had established that.' He smiled coldly. 'I am your husband.'

'In name only,' Leigh lashed back quickly as her heartbeat raced.

'I'm quite prepared to rectify that if you'd care to oblige?' His eyes were mocking. 'I seem to remember we were good together once.' The blue eyes were insultingly familiar.

'We were?' Her mouth curled scornfully. 'Are you sure it was us you are thinking of? There have been so many women in your life, Raoul, I'm surprised you can remember any one liaison.'

At last she had hit him on the raw. She saw it in the arctic frost that turned the vivid blue eyes rapier-sharp and the way his big body froze into stillness. 'You were not a ''liaison'', Leigh,' he said furiously. 'You were, you *are*, my wife!'

'It was a pity you didn't remember that when it counted,' she said simply. 'Goodbye, Raoul.'

She had turned and left him before he realised what was happening and as she crossed the room she half expected to feel a restraining hand on her shoulder but nothing happened. She wanted to run away, to find a safe little hidey-hole where she could lick the wounds that she'd thought had healed but which were as raw as the day he had gouged them into her heart—but she wouldn't give him the satisfaction. How had he found her? Why was he here? More to the point, why was she here?

She looked through the high, beautifully worked arched doorway into the next massive room full of London's élite—high society at its best, with the odd bearded aesthete to keep Nigel's precious balance right—and groaned inwardly. When she had first begun to be noticed, two years ago, she had decided then that the power game was not for her. She would succeed or fail on her paintings, not on her connections, but when the prized invitation had dropped through her letterbox she had been unable to resist. The urge to see first-hand one of Nigel's famous soirées had been too tempting. Curiosity! Well, now she was paying for her weakness in a way she had never anticipated in her darkest nightmares.

'Everything all right, sweetie?' As Nigel drifted by without waiting for an answer, his long sequinned smock in outrageous contrast to the tight bright red trousers, she bit her lip hard. She had been here two hours. She had been seen by the right people and now she couldn't stand it another minute. A careful glance backwards told her Raoul was nowhere to be seen, now was the moment to escape. She had to get away, break free.

'Off already, darling?' She was just slipping into
her jacket, incongruous against the mass of furs
and silk shawls that filled the rest of the ladies'
cloakroom, when Vivien's smooth white hand
touched her arm imperiously. 'Bigger fish to fry?'

'I beg your pardon?' Leigh had never liked
Vivien, having had the misfortune to work with her
on more than one occasion in her early days in
London when she was working part-time as a pho-
tographer's assistant in order to be able to eat while
she followed her dream to paint, and now she
turned to face the taller woman with frank distaste
on her heart-shaped face. 'I don't understand.'

'I just bet you don't.' Vivien's hard slanted eyes
were poisonous. 'What's your little game, then? I've
made a few enquiries and that's Raoul de Chevnair
you were talking to, isn't it? You don't seriously
expect me to believe that a multimillionaire playboy
like Raoul de Chevnair would ever notice a little
nobody like you, let alone marry her!' She laughed
spitefully, her face mocking.

'I don't expect you to believe anything, Vivien,'
Leigh said coldly, her shoulders straight and her
face mirroring her opinion of the beautiful blonde
more effectively than words ever could have done.
'Now would you mind moving out of the way? I'm
going home.' Her voice was glacial.

'Yes, I would mind, actually,' Vivien drawled
slowly, her mouth pulled into a thin red line and
her eyes shooting daggers. 'You haven't answered
my question, Miss Leigh Wilson! Doesn't sound
much like Mrs de Chevnair to me!'

'Then, as my husband said a few minutes ago, that's your problem.' Leigh pushed past the willowy figure, taking her completely by surprise. 'Goodnight, Vivien.'

Once outside the cloakroom in the large wood-panelled hall, she leant against the wall for a moment and took a deep breath. Already! Raoul had only been back in her life five minutes and already the women were gathering like bees round a honeypot. But he wasn't back in her life! She seized on the thought and repeated it to herself firmly. She wouldn't let him be.

When she had crawled from his presence, crushed and broken, all those years ago, she had felt that life was a deep black abyss that would never hold a spark of joy or contentment again. And it hadn't at first. She had fled back to London, hiding herself in the careless anonymity of the big metropolis, unable to think or eat or sleep for weeks—and then one spring morning a ray of sunshine had caught a spider's web on the window of her grubby little bedsit and the urge to paint had resurfaced. And with it she had gradually clawed back her self-respect, making a new life for herself, taking charge of her affairs, growing into a person whom, if she didn't actually like, she could live with. And over the years she had settled into the new woman who had been reborn out of the scorching devastation, content with her light sunny little flat with its bird's-eye view of London and her peaceful solitary life. A tranquil life in the cool valley after the cruel heat of the mountaintop. And now he was back! Her heart pounded so violently for a moment that she felt faint. Why—after all this time? She had made it clear to him when she'd left that everything between them had been burnt to ashes, that there was nothing left. So why now, just when everything was beginning to happen for her?

She levered herself carefully off the wall and walked sedately to the heavily carved oak front door, opening it quietly and slipping through quickly with a sigh of relief that she had got away so easily. She felt shell-shocked, bruised.

The warm summer air was filled with the city perfume of petrol fumes and dirt but she didn't care; she had got used to London in all its moods now, appreciating the obscurity of town life, the nameless oblivion, hugging it to her like a hard-won prize. She was just Leigh Wilson, budding artist; that was all.

The night was black without a shred of moonlight to lighten the darkness, and the old-fashioned wrought-iron street lamps gave a discreetly small circle of light into the elegant, quiet, expensive avenue. As she stepped down the narrow circular steps into the empty street she clucked disapprovingly to herself. She should have called for a taxi before she left. She wasn't thinking straight, but then it was hardly surprising!

'Leigh?' As one of the tall shadows across the dimly lit expanse detached itself she gave a little start of surprise, swiftly concealed, and then she was staring into Raoul's dark face again and he wasn't smiling. 'Can I give you a lift?' He indicated a long, low, sleek white monster on wheels a few yards away. 'Please?'

Please? This wasn't the Raoul she knew. The Raoul she had lived with for eighteen glorious, mind-boggling months had never said please to anyone in his life. 'I don't think so.' She stared at him nervously. 'I don't want to be difficult, but——'

'Then don't be.' As he cut into her words the arrogant forcefulness curled the muscles in her stomach. *This* was the Raoul she knew, riding roughshod over everyone else, cutting through any small talk, intent only on getting his own way. The veneer was just that—a light covering to hide a mind of steel. 'I intend to talk to you, Leigh, so you might as well get it over and done with now.' He smiled coldly. 'You never were one for putting off unpleasant duties, were you?'

There was something of the satyr about him, she thought painfully; there always had been. Perhaps that was what had attracted her once, but not any more! Now she could see him for exactly what he was and it disgusted her.

'Is it really necessary?' She still didn't move from the last step. 'Can't our solicitors sort it out?'

'No, they damn well can't!' He took a long deep breath and spoke more quietly. 'I don't want solicitors meddling in my affairs. Now be a good girl and come and talk to me for a few minutes while I take you home. Kingston Gardens, isn't it?'

She looked at him in surprise and took a step forwards in spite of herself. 'How do you know where I live?'

'I told you, I know more about you than you think,' he said smoothly, his deep rich voice and faint accent giving the words a sensual overtone that brought the blood rushing into her cheeks. 'First it was a bedsit in Baron Place, then a shared flat with a Miss...' the dark brows wrinkled '...ah, yes, a Miss Angela Hardwick, and for the last two years a flat of your own in Kingston Gardens.' He folded muscled arms.

'Have you been spying on me?' she asked weakly. 'I don't believe this.' A flood of burning anger replaced the stunned amazement his words had caused. 'How dare you? How *dare* you, Raoul? I——'

'Shut up and get in the car,' he said brusquely, the patience for which he was not renowned running out suddenly. As he took hold of her arm a shiver of apprehension trembled down her spine—or was it excitement? She bit on her lower lip till it hurt. She mustn't let him see how he affected her. She hated and loathed him but he might mistake it for something else. She would listen to what he said, coolly and calmly, and then that would be that. And he was right. She might as well get it over and done with now.

The interior of the car was as magnificent as the outside, soft white leather seats and thick grey carpet, a sexual experience on wheels, she thought balefully. How in keeping. How *very* in keeping!

'Do take that frown of disapproval off your face,' he said lazily as he joined her. 'You'll have deep lines before you're forty at this rate and I don't intend to spend a fortune on face-lifts as you get older. My wife will grow old gracefully.'

'What?' She swung round to face him, big brown eyes incredulous, hardly able to believe what she had heard. 'What on earth are you talking about?'

'Us,' he replied easily. 'I'm talking about us.' He urged the big car into purring life, drawing out of the parking space and joining the main stream of traffic at the end of the avenue, seemingly totally relaxed and faintly amused.

'There is no "us",' she said sharply as she turned to look out of the window at the brightly lit shops and restaurants they were passing at incredible speed. He was driving too fast but then he always had. It had been a mistake to get in the car. The big, powerful, muscular body so close to hers was bringing back too many unwelcome memories, memories that caused her cheeks to burn and her eyes to glitter as she sternly repressed the aching fluttering in the pit of her stomach. He even smelt the same! That delicious and wickedly expensive aftershave that had always rendered her helpless in his arms. She brought her knees together tightly. She was immune to him now. She was!

'Oh, but there is, kitten.' The use of the old pet name jarred piercingly into her heart. 'There always will be.'

'I want to get out.' Her hands were clenched together now and she ground her teeth silently as a low laugh rippled through the car. 'Do you hear me, Raoul?'

'No way, my love.' She steeled herself to look at him and then wished she hadn't. The profile was so familiar, so devastingly, painfully familiar. She had forgotten just how breathtakingly handsome he was, how enigmatically in control, how altogether electric. It wasn't fair that one man should have so much going for him. It wasn't just his looks, compelling though they were; there was a dark magnetism, an inner vitality that accentuated every aspect of the lean hard body and tanned face until the aura in which he moved was all-absorbing. 'You're nearly home now.'

Even as he spoke he pulled off the main thoroughfare which led to the huge block of flats where she lived and into a narrow, deserted side-street that was dark and unlit. 'Now then.' As the engine died a sense of danger shivered down her spine. This was Raoul, Raoul her husband, the man who knew her more intimately than any other human being ever would, the man who had almost destroyed her once and had let her go almost casually. The feeling of exhilaration that had had her in its grip since the party died, and pure un-diluted fear took its place. Was she strong enough to withstand his devious fascination now? She had never understood him and had no idea why he had sought her out after all this time but she sensed instinctively that it wasn't an impulsive decision.

She had been right in her initial impression that he had changed. The old Raoul had never had such a hard light of cold purpose in his eyes. He was the same but he was different: older, menacingly determined, altogether more dangerous. She prepared herself for what he was going to say. Whatever it was, she wouldn't like it, she was suddenly quite sure of that.

'Leigh . . .' As he spoke her name he bent towards her, the fingers of one hand threading into her thick silky hair as the other wrapped round her waist, drawing her into him in the close confines of the car before she had time to resist.

'Don't!' Even as she spoke his mouth took hers and in the first moment of contact she knew, with a frantic silent scream, that the old magic was there. She couldn't evade him, there was nowhere to go, and, bent over her as he was, his body had trapped her more securely than any chains. The kiss shot through the nerve-endings all over her body in an explosion of sensation, moulding, drawing her, emptying her of everything but him. She tried to fight it, to jerk her head away, but he was too strong for her and then, as the kiss became deeper and he plundered that intimate territory she had never given to anyone else but him, she didn't want to resist. The dizzy, helpless submission his passion had always induced rose like a phoenix from the ashes, sensual, powerful, accelerating her heartbeat and causing her to strain towards him, revelling in the feel, the smell of him as he fitted her into his body until she could feel every inch of his hard frame.

She couldn't believe she had been without the touch, the feel of him for five years. Like an addict who thought she had conquered the habit only to find its pull stronger than ever, she shuddered desperately against him, his obvious arousal firing her to new heights of ecstasy.

He seemed gripped by the same sort of madness, murmuring incoherently against the softness of her mouth, his lips moving frantically over her face and throat as his body trembled against hers, a storm of pent-up emotion devouring the long lean body until the tremors that were shaking his limbs reached through to hers.

'You're mine, you're still mine, you'll always be mine...' As his voice, urgent and filled with a mad exultation, pierced the spinning whirlwind that had her in its grip, she froze in his arms, a biting wave of humiliation and shame breaking over her head and draining the colour from her face.

'No!' As she wrenched her face from his she jerked sideways savagely, hitting her shoulder against the door of the car without even feeling it. It wasn't going to happen again. She wasn't going to be swept into his orbit like a mindless robot that could only function when its master pressed the switch. She was autonomous now, she didn't need him any more, she *wouldn't* need him! She had survived without him for five years; it couldn't all be lost now. She had to fight him.

'Leigh, listen to me——'

'No!' She knew she was almost hysterical but that didn't matter, all that mattered was convincing him that he had to leave her alone, that she was her own person now, not a plaything to be brought out at convenient moments. 'Don't you touch me again, Raoul, not ever again. I mean it, I hate you! I'll always hate you!' She was shouting and in the enclosed space the words bounced off the metal with deafening ferocity, and as she struggled to open the door she was aware of him leaning back into his seat, his face hardening into cold mocking lines.

'A simple "no" would have sufficed,' he said quietly. 'You really didn't have to pretend that you enjoyed what was obviously a grievous ordeal.' He was laughing at her! In the same instant that the mocking words registered on her bruised mind her hand shot out with savage force to hit him hard across one tanned cheek, the sound deafening.

'Leigh!' He punched her name into the space between them as his hands shot up to hold hers, restraining her with just enough force for the mad pounding in her head to ease and the enormity of what she had just done to break into her consciousness. She shut her eyes against the look on his face, leaning back against the soft leather as she felt the strength drain from her body, leaving her quivering and silent. 'Consider yourself most fortunate,' he grated through tight-clenched teeth. 'There is no other woman on this earth who would get away with that twice.'

Twice? As her eyes opened to meet his the memory of their last encounter was there as clearly as if it was yesterday. Marion's long, golden loose-limbed body sprawled on the bed—their bed—her long golden blonde hair spread out across the pillow like a silky veil and the big green eyes bright with triumph as they caught sight of her standing white-faced in the doorway. Her clothes had been scattered round the bedroom floor as though discarded in a frenzied game of tag, and as Raoul had emerged from the *en suite*, magnificently and in the circumstances inexcusably naked, she knew with a sick feeling of despair exactly who the beautiful blonde had been playing with.

'Leigh?' Raoul had begun to speak, his eyes flying from her drowning eyes to Marion in one lightning glance, but she had blown his words away with the impact of her hand across his mouth. She shut her mind to the scene that had followed. She had dissected it too often as it was.

'I'll take you home.' As her eyes refocused on his face he let go of her hands, placing them into her lap as though she was old and helpless, which was exactly how she felt. She had been almost twenty when she had left him. After eighteen months of heaven on earth she had been plunged into a dark void that was indescribable, and just for a minute, a crazy minute, she had forgotten that tonight. But never again.

She glanced at him as he manoeuvred the powerful car out of the narrow street and into the lights again. This time her head must, *must* rule her heart! She couldn't let herself become this man's plaything again, his little toy. She was a grown woman now, not a child bride; she had shaped and woven her own life into the pattern she required of it and her independence was the most precious thing she owned.

I hate you, Raoul, she said silently as the car purred its way through the traffic, I hate you, I do! So why was it that for the first time in five years she felt alive again?

CHAPTER TWO

'I'LL see you to your door.' Leigh's heart was still pounding with disgust at her own weakness as they drew up outside the block of flats where she lived, and as his cool expressionless voice cut into her whirling thoughts she stiffened instinctively, her eyes widening in protest.

'No!' She lowered her voice a few decibels and tried again. 'No, Raoul, please don't.'

'As you wish.' He was sitting very still, an intense watchfulness colouring his eyes ice-blue. 'Goodnight, Leigh.'

'What? Oh, goodnight.' This was it, then? After five years? A macabre anticlimax was making her knees weak.

As she climbed out of the car it was gone in an instant, roaring down the street to the blaring of horns and screaming brakes from the other traffic, the sound of its engine soon lost in the general mêlée.

As the lift took her upwards she really felt as though she was going to collapse. Her legs felt like jelly and there was a strange blackness that was most peculiar coming and going in front of her eyes. She suddenly realised she was leaning against the wall of the lift, which was unsavoury at the best of times, and on a Saturday evening, after the revelry and beer-swilling carousal of a Friday night, definitely suspect.

It brought her back to earth abruptly and she even found herself smiling at the irony of leaving Raoul's fabulously expensive car to step into such a paradoxical little box. She shrugged wearily. Such was life. If only Raoul were as easy to shrug away.

The little flat was cool and welcoming as she opened her front door. One of the advantages of being on the sixth floor was that she could leave the large French doors that took up almost one wall of the tiny lounge open in the summer, letting the cool night air and rich scents from the tiny balcony crammed full with potted plants and sweet-smelling tubs of bright flowers stream into the room. She used this room as a small studio; the light was excellent all year round, and the minute tiled bathroom leading off the small box bedroom and even tinier kitchen kept housework to a minimum.

She owned one comfortable old easy-chair parked at one side of the windows, one bed and a small wardrobe, and that was all the furniture she possessed, having ploughed all her money into the hundreds of pounds' worth of canvases, paints and brushes that roamed across every inch of available space, cluttering the walls in untidy harmony and filling the flat with the smell of turpentine and paint. And she loved it. She stood for a moment feasting her eyes on her little domain, willing the hard-won peace and quiet contentment back into her heart. But it was no good. She grimaced to herself helplessly. Raoul had destroyed it, at least for tonight. She wouldn't let it be any longer than that!

She was standing under the shower, letting the cool water annihilate the last flush of humiliation still staining her skin pink, when the telephone called stridently from its hook on the kitchen wall. 'You can just ring,' she told it loudly, reaching for the bottle of shampoo and pouring a large amount of the thick creamy mixture into her hair, working up a lather determinedly.

She couldn't speak to anyone tonight, she just couldn't. Her head was swimming with a thousand and one images, her mind was aching and she *still* didn't know why Raoul had exploded back into her life! The phone rang again as she was towelling herself dry and once more as she lay in bed sipping a hot mug of cocoa and flicking through a magazine article on life drawing by one of her old lecturers at college. It had become a matter of principle not to answer it now, a kind of rebellion against having the frame of her carefully built screen of fragile self-sufficiency broken by Raoul's easy intrusion.

Sleep was too long in coming and she didn't have the patience to wait for it, preferring paint and canvas after an hour of tossing and turning and forcing her mind away from paths that it dared not follow. Delectable, forbidden paths where Raoul's magnificent body was exposed in all its flagrant manhood and her shape was moulded into his in a manner as old as time. The phone was now off the hook; that, at least, she could control! She had another cool shower before she started work at two o'clock. The night was excessively warm, she told herself aggressively—that was *absolutely* all it was!

At six she fell into bed just as she was, paint-smeared and somewhat grubby, and at eight o'clock she was woken by a furious pounding at her front door that she was sure could be heard on the tenth floor.

She stumbled bleary-eyed to the door, still in her tattered old painting smock, her hair tangled and hanging limply on her shoulders and her eyes cloudy with lack of sleep.

'And just where the hell have you been?'

'What?' Raoul's face was a picture of injured outrage and for a moment she wondered if she was in the middle of some inexplicable nightmare. 'What are you doing here?'

'Answer me, damn you!' He seemed very angry, she reflected weakly as she tried to spark her mind into ignition. 'I've been ringing this number most of the night. First there was no answer and then it was engaged. What are you playing at? Who have you got here?' His voice was bitingly sharp.

'Who have I . . . ?' He brushed past her into the flat, stalking into each tiny room before coming to a halt in front of her stained easel, the paint on the canvas still tacky.

'You've been working all night, haven't you? You took the phone off the hook because you were working. You stupid girl!' He glared at her angrily. 'What about an emergency? What if someone was trying to get you urgently?'

'Stop shouting at me!' She had found her tongue along with the burning resentment that was filling her small body from head to foot. 'And what did that gibe mean, incidentally? "Who have I got here?" You cheeky hound! We aren't all like you, Raoul. Some of us consider that there are more important things than procreational pursuits!'

'What?' In a more conventional situation the look of sheer amazement on Raoul's face would have been food for her soul, but just at the moment she couldn't appreciate that for once she had totally and completely surprised him.

'You burst into my home, you accuse me of goodness knows what and then you criticise my lifestyle! How dare you? *How dare you*? You haven't bothered with me for five years and now you think you can tell me what to do. Get out! *Get out*!'

'"Procreational pursuits"?' He didn't even seem to have heard the rest of her tirade. '"Procreational pursuits"!' The great peal of unbridled raucous laughter took her completely by surprise. Raoul laughed the way he did everything else, with unrestrained frankness and wholehearted participation, and in spite of the fact that it was eight o'clock on a Sunday morning and the neighbours would be thinking—well, she didn't dare to imagine what they *would* be thinking—she found herself infected by his appreciation of the moment. Unfortunately they had always had the same slightly off-beat sense of humour. It had seemed good when they were together but as Mrs Billett next door banged ferociously on the wall and Mr Silver overhead nearly brought the ceiling down with his walking-stick, she tried to restrain the paroxysms of laughter that recurred every time she thought she had control. It was nerves, it had to be.

'Oh, Leigh...' Raoul had collapsed on the one and only chair and was looking at her through streaming eyes. 'Only you could come out with a phrase like that. "Procreational pursuits"!' His head went back in another burst of laughter. 'You're priceless, kitten, you really are.'

Somehow the nickname sobered them both at the same moment and from helpless laughter they changed to expectant stillness within seconds. 'Leigh?' Raoul's voice was a low endearment and she shuddered against it, her hands going out in unconscious protest as she took a step backwards. 'Let me hold you, show you nothing has really changed.'

'No, no, Raoul...' He crossed the room in one movement to stand looking down at her, small and defenceless, in front of his overpoweringly tall bulk, and then with a smothered groan he lifted her right off her feet into his arms.

'You've got paint on your nose and you stink of turpentine,' he said softly as he traced the outline of her jaw with tiny feather-light kisses, his lips moving to her mouth as she opened it to protest. 'And you're so damn beautiful...' Why that word should be the catalyst to the emotion that was sending hot waves of desire into every nerve-ending she didn't know. Maybe it was because no one else had ever called her beautiful, maybe it was because the images she had been fighting all night had reared their sensual heads as soon as she had seen his face again. Whatever, she was now fighting herself as much as him and she was suddenly scared to death.

'Put me down, Raoul! I don't want this, I don't want you——' As he smothered her voice with a piercingly sweet kiss the feel of his hard, warm lips brought a host of memories she was powerless to resist. Raoul, the frighteningly perceptive lover who had been as anxious for her satisfaction as his own, infinitely patient, incredibly tender but capable of such heights of erotic passion that she had frequently felt she would die from the glorious ecstasy he induced.

He had been her first love, her only love, and had constantly delighted in fusing their bodies into rapturous oblivion until she had been quivering and sated in his arms. This was the Raoul she had purposely blocked out of her consciousness for years in her desire to survive, drawing on the mental picture of a cold hard womaniser who had betrayed her in the most callous way possible and with seemingly no shred of remorse.

'I want you, my darling.' How they had reached the bed she didn't know—she hadn't been aware that he had carried her there as she had continued to struggle against the seductive weakness that was flooding her limbs at his touch—but as he laid her down on the rumpled covers she brought every ounce of will-power she possessed into play. It couldn't happen again, she couldn't let him take her over again.

'Leave me alone, Raoul.' Her eyes were huge as she stared up at him in the dim light from the curtained window. 'I can't——'

'But you can, kitten! We're married, Leigh; you're my wife, remember?' His voice was teasingly mocking as he stroked a silky lock of brown hair away from her face with a gentle hand, lazily leaning forward to take her lips with his own again.

He was so sure of himself, she thought with a little dart of pain that strengthened her resolve. So sure that he could overcome her resistance as though the last five years had meant nothing! But then, they probably hadn't to him! Had he even noticed she'd gone? She froze into stillness as he kissed her again, forcing her senses into submission and willing the warm pulsing beat of desire that was making her limbs shake to quieten. He didn't notice her lack of response at first, and as he continued to trace a path of fire over her face and throat she knew it was only a matter of time before the heat that was bursting into life deep inside became evident again. She clenched her hands tightly by her side. She had to make him stop and this was the only way. She had to find the strength from somewhere.

Her complete lack of movement finally got through to him and he raised himself slowly, leaning on one elbow at her side to look into her wide brown eyes as he raked back the shock of curly black hair from his brow. 'Don't tell me I'm losing my touch?' The dry, sardonic tone whipped a flush of colour into her cheeks and fanned the earlier flame of pain into white-hot agony.

With a bitterness that was directed at herself as well as him she stiffened into stone in an effort to hide the hurt. He really didn't care! 'Losing your touch?' Her voice dripped with contempt. 'Is that all anything means to you? An opportunity to prove you're the greatest? That no woman is immune?' Mercifully anger was replacing the pain now.

If she hadn't been so angry she would have taken warning at the slow darkening of his face but right at that moment she was incapable of taking notice of anything. 'You disgust me, Raoul, with your arrogant and all-important male ego. We're strangers now and you know it! We're just two people held together by a meaningless piece of paper.'

'Like hell we are!' He swung his legs violently over the edge of the bed as he turned from her. 'Was that why you insisted on a church wedding because all our marriage boiled down to was an expendable bit of paper? I do not believe this, Leigh; I know you better than that. You are my wife, *my wife* in the eyes of God and man, and I know it and so do you.' His accent was as brittle as glass.

'No——'

'Oh, yes, my little English rose.' He stood up as she drew herself into a sitting position, locking her hands round her knees after pulling the short smock down to her feet. 'You are mine and what is mine I keep. You should know this.' His voice was shaking with rage and cold determination.

'Raoul, listen to me——'

'Why should I?' He spun round now with a dark raging fury in his eyes that made her shrink away in fear. '*You* do not listen to *me*, do you? You didn't listen five years ago and still you will not. What is it with you?'

'What is it with *me*?' The sheer arrogance acted like a shot of adrenalin and her small face was convulsed with hot resentment and burning fury. 'How can you ask me that? You aren't real! You just aren't real.'

'This is nonsense,' he said coldly, his face hard and his eyes an icy blue. 'If you cannot talk sense——'

'Can't talk sense!' He had turned into the iceman again but for the life of her she couldn't match his coolness. He stood gazing at her, powerfully, dangerously handsome with an insolent tilt to the ebony head and his eyes such a startling vivid blue that her breath suddenly caught in her throat as she fought for words. He was so handsome. So amazingly, painfully handsome. What had he ever seen in her anyway? 'I may not be saying what you want to hear but it makes perfect sense, to me at any rate.' Her voice was trembling and low and she heard it with a little throb of self-disgust. She wouldn't let him break her, reduce her to tears again.

He swore softly as he took in the huge brown eyes in her chalk-white face, filled with a churning darkness that made him run his hand through his hair wearily, the anger draining from his face as he shook his head gently. 'You are your own worst enemy, kitten,' he said softly. 'We were so good together once and you cannot deny we were happy. You can't fight what's between us, Leigh; your body betrays you every time I touch you. You want me to make love to you.'

For a stunned moment she couldn't believe what she was hearing, couldn't believe he could have the audacity to actually voice such incredible words in view of what he had done. 'You betrayed me, Raoul.' Her voice was flat now and totally devoid of expression. 'In the worst possible way. In our own bed. You can't deny that.'

'I cannot?' His eyes narrowed slowly and his voice was very tight, his body stiff with emotion. 'But of course I cannot. It is all cut and dried, is it not? Like that evening five years ago when I wasn't allowed to speak?'

'Oh, and I suppose if you'd come back to our home and found me in bed with another man you would have sat down with us in a reasonable manner and asked politely for an explanation?' She glared at him. 'There was only one possible interpretation. Admit it!'

'You weary me.' His face had hardened further at the note of undisguised disgust in her voice.

'*I* weary *you*?' She was aware in the far recesses of her mind that she kept repeating his remarks like a dozy parrot, but the haughty insolence was leaving her gasping for words. 'Well, maybe I do at that. But I'm not stupid and I won't pretend to be. Marion had been after you for weeks and you knew it. I suppose you only held out for as long as you did because she was your best friend's wife and they were staying with us. You betrayed him and me and for what? A little——' She stopped abruptly and took a long deep breath, settling back into the bed and pulling the covers more closely around her. She felt suddenly cold, cold and very tired. 'Anyway, it's over, finished; none of it matters any more. Maybe we can be friends one day.' She missed the lightning flash of pain in his face.

'I do not want friendship from you,' he said savagely. 'I want more, much more than that or nothing at all.'

'Then it will be nothing,' she said slowly as she lifted her eyes to stare straight into the arctic blue of his.

'You think so?' His voice was soft now and with a chilling coldness that sent a tiny shiver sparking down her spine. She knew Raoul. He was always at his most dangerous when perfectly in control like now. 'Tell me, my Leigh, what did you imagine would happen in the future? Did you seriously expect me to remain in the background like an emasculated stallion forever?' She shivered at the crudity.

'I didn't expect anything,' she said tightly, forcing her eyes not to fall before the piercing clarity of his. 'I didn't expect anything and I don't *want* anything. Not from you. I thought you knew that after all this time.'

'Then this is where you are wrong,' he said calmly as he walked easily towards the door, his big shoulders proudly straight and his head held high. 'Quite wrong.'

'Can't you just leave me alone, Raoul——?'

He spun round instantly with that smooth animal reflex she remembered from the past. She could tell he was angry, blazingly angry, but the big body was held in quiet restraint and his voice was perfectly contained when he next spoke.

'No, I will not leave you alone any more.' It was a statement rather than a threat but it had the same effect on her as the latter. She couldn't understand any of this. What exactly did he want of her after all these years? 'We have things to decide and arrangements to make but I refuse to discuss it now. Not with you in this mood.'

'This "mood" is me,' she said sharply, 'and nothing you could say would convince me——'

He cut off her words with a vicious stab of his hand as he waved her to silence from the doorway. 'I have given you the time you asked for that day when you left, the chance to follow your dream of becoming an artist, the opportunity to become your own person, but that doesn't mean that I will allow anyone else to take my place. Do you understand me?' He glared at her across the small room, his hands arrogantly splayed on his hips and his eyes flashing cold fire. 'If I had kept you with me you would never have been sure of what you could have achieved, never sure if your love for me was a mirage that had chained you to my side.'

She stared at him silently as she tried to take in what he was saying. This was all nonsense. She hadn't said——

'I have never been more than a step behind you through the years. I have known exactly what you were doing, what you were involved with, who you were seeing and when. And this Jeff Capstone, I will not tolerate that you see him. Is that clear?'

She still couldn't speak, couldn't formulate what she was hearing——

'I shall return to see you tomorrow and I will tell you then how I expect you to behave. Goodbye, Leigh.'

'Raoul!' As she found her tongue the front door slammed with a violence that rocked the tiny flat and as she went to leap out of bed to follow him, her cheeks scarlet with anger, she caught her bare foot in the bedclothes and fell in a sprawling heap on to the floor. By the time she reached the front door the lift's ancient whirring mechanism informed her she was too late. He had gone.

As she slowly stepped back in the flat, shutting the door, her rage grew in tune with her sense of injustice. It was as though they had been talking about a different marriage and two different people! She ground her teeth furiously. She had left him because she had found him in bed with another woman! End of story. What was all this rubbish about time and being her own person? And he had had her followed! She paced the small flat angrily. He had *actually* had the audacity to have her followed!

She made herself a cup of instant coffee in order to give her shaking hands something to do, wandering out on to the small balcony as she sipped the hot liquid and looking out over the rooftops into the clear blue sky.

If he contacted her again, *when* he contacted her again, she was going to insist on that divorce. She closed her eyes tightly. She had to sever all links, all ties; she should have done it years ago. Why hadn't she? She opened her eyes to gaze unseeing into the warm summer air. Because she had been hanging on to a dream against all reason. She had pushed the divorce out of her mind, not because she didn't want to think of Raoul but because she dared not!

She brushed back the heavy fall of hair from her face and took a big gulp of coffee, letting the burning liquid trace an avenue of fire into her chest. In those heady days of marriage she had dreamt of their life together as being for always, of their babies, their grandchildren. She smiled bitterly to herself. But it had just been part of the impossible dream and she'd had to let go of it before it destroyed her. It hadn't been real. Their life together hadn't been real.

She leant against the wrought iron, which was already slightly warm from the heat of the summer's day, as dark misery gripped her mind. Raoul's wealth had cocooned them in an endless honeymoon. First a few months at his beautiful house in the Caribbean, eight weeks at his villa in Greece and then a long, slow cruise on his private yacht to the house he called home in the South of France.

It had been miraculous and magical—but it hadn't been real. Real life was working and caring and loving and taking the rough with the smooth. It had been all smoothness. And it was finished.

As she turned to go back into the room she noticed a tiny tentacled weed in a tub of wallflowers in the corner of the balcony and suddenly its intrusion seemed symbolic of Raoul's reappearance in her life. As she pulled it, viciously, from the black earth she nodded to herself desperately as the flood of tears she could no longer restrain burnt hot on her face. It *was* finished. It had to be.

CHAPTER THREE

'MRS DE CHEVNAIR?' The young lad standing outside her door was almost buried under the huge bouquet of deep red roses he was holding. 'Mrs Leigh de Chevnair?'

'Yes?' Leigh's voice was grudging. To be woken up on a Monday morning at nine o'clock when she hadn't slept all night and then asked to acknowledge her married status wasn't her idea of a good start to the week.

'I thought I'd got the address right but the card on the door says Leigh Wilson.' The boy's forehead was wrinkled. 'Still, that's your affair.'

'Exactly.' She wasn't usually this snappy, she thought miserably as she reluctantly took charge of the flowers that could only be from one person as the boy left with a stiff nod. She had to get herself together! There was no card, just the picture of a small brown kitten fixed to the enormous silk bow at the base of the bouquet, its eyes enormous.

She deposited the flowers in the kitchen sink before having a shower and getting dressed, her movements mechanical and slow. The memories that had haunted her all night were just as vivid in the cold light of day and as she brushed her hair in the bathroom mirror she peered at herself critically for the first time in months.

The anxious face that stared back at her was averagely pretty, no more, she reflected miserably, the big brown eyes and thick dark hair pleasant but fairly mediocre. Her shape was inclined to plumpness, she wasn't very tall and yet from the first moment they had met Raoul had called her beautiful.

She peered closer, trying to see what he saw, but after a few searching moments shook her head in defeat. Oh, Raoul ... 'Now none of that,' she told herself loudly. 'It's over, finished! You are going to devote yourself to your work and become a great artist.' The thought couldn't have depressed her more and after a few minutes of claustrophobic misery she decided she had to get out and go for a walk. She needed to get her hopes and aspirations back on course and she couldn't do it with the smell of fifty or more roses pervading her senses and weakening her resolve.

'Running away? Again?' The bright warm sunlight trapped neatly in the building-framed street had momentarily blinded her as she stepped out on to the pavement from the dark confines of the murky passageway leading from the lift, and as she raised startled brown eyes to Raoul's cool sardonic face she almost groaned out loud. He had no right to look so gorgeous, no right at all. Dressed simply in figure-hugging jeans and a blue denim shirt that reflected the deep blue of his eyes, he looked ... gorgeous. But he wasn't hers. Not any more.

'I happen to be going for a walk...if that's all right with you, of course.' She smiled tightly. 'I'll be back in an hour. My clocking-in card is in my pocket.'

'Miaow...' He touched her flushed cheek gently with a cool finger. 'My little kitten is scratchy today.' She glared at him without replying and he laughed softly. 'I think I'll join you; I need the exercise.'

Now she did groan out loud, and he eyed her quizzically as he fell into step beside her. 'It's lucky for me I do not suffer with the English insecurity,' he said quietly. 'You have been death to my ego from the first moment we met.' He placed a casual arm round her shoulders and she saw two beautifully dressed career women across the road grimace with envy. She didn't have to be able to hear what they were saying to know its content; she'd heard it so many times before. 'What a dish! And what's he doing with her?'

'Do you remember?' he continued softly in her ear as he moderated his large steps to hers. 'In St Tropez?'

'Of course I remember,' she said painfully. 'I was on a cheap package holiday with my cousin and you were on your yacht with Lord Somebody-or-other.' She eyed him morosely. 'Very symbolic!' He ignored the gibe with regal indifference. 'And then you started to show off on the beach for all the women.'

'I did not!' Now she had his attention! 'I merely played football with a group of friends, that is all.'

He shot her a warning glance. 'You are not too big to fit over my knee, little kitten, understand?' Now she ignored him. 'And there was one girl who would not emerge from her umbrella. Buried up to her nose in her newspaper. Just a pair of round dimpled knees on view.' He smiled slowly. 'I fell for those knees then and there.' The blue eyes were reflective.

'Raoul!' She pushed him slightly with her hand as she fought, unsuccessfully, to keep back the grin that was twisting the corners of her mouth upwards. She shouldn't listen to this.

'Oh, but I did.' His eyes narrowed in remembrance. 'And then, when I persuaded the butterfly from its chrysalis, it was to find that I was—how you say?—cradle-snatching.'

'You were not,' she said indignantly. 'I was eighteen when we met and you were only twenty-five. Not exactly Methuselah by anyone's standards!'

'Ah, but you were a baby in the ways of love,' he said deeply. 'But how quickly you learnt. You will always be mine, Leigh, you know this?' She couldn't quite place the timbre of his voice but there was something in the hard handsome face that was quite ruthless and she shivered in spite of the heat.

'Like your car or yacht, you mean?' Her voice was deliberately cold. 'Something to be used when necessary or convenient and then put into the appropriate slot or maybe even forgotten if a better model comes along.' She looked straight up at him now. 'Maybe another Marion?'

'You say these things but you do not believe them,' he said grimly as he brought her to a halt at the opening of a tiny green park with a pocket handkerchief square of lawn surrounded by a border of orderly bushes and regimented benches. 'Marriage is forever. There has never been a divorce in my family.'

'Is that all that matters to you? Your family's reputation?'

He brought her angry words to a halt by the simple expèdient of placing his lips on hers, bending down to take her mouth with an arrogant gesture of familiarity that had her head jerking away immediately. She ignored the response the casual action ignited in her body, veiling her eyes against him as she glared up into his face. 'Don't.'

'I have decided there is only one way to deal with your stubbornness, kitten,' he said thoughtfully. 'I have given you time to to find yourself, to become established in your work. I let this happen because I had to. Now it is time for you to come back to me.'

'You're crazy.' She stared at him in amazement. 'I'm not coming back, Raoul.'

'This person, this Jeff, does he have something to do with your decision?' he asked coldly as he drew her down beside him on one of the benches, his touch burning her arm.

'My life is my own affair now,' she said quietly as a dart of anger at his presumption turned her eyes black. 'You don't own me any more.'

'I never did.' He looked down at her quizzically. 'I never wanted to "own" you in that way. Possess you, as you possess me, maybe, but not "own" you.'

'We're finished.' She had said it! She shut her eyes for an infinitesimal moment of time, expecting another explosion, but apart from a stiffening of the big body there was no change in his manner. He sat watching her, his blue eyes reflecting the sky overhead and the faint breeze ruffling his hair. This was merely a game to him, she thought wretchedly.

'Did you like the roses?' he asked with cool detachment. She stared at him for a moment, nonplussed by his control.

'They're lovely.' She smiled nervously. 'You must have bought the shop out.' What on earth did he expect her to say?

'A rose for every month we have been apart.' There was no expression in the smooth voice. 'How are you going to convince me you are adamant our marriage is at an end?' he asked in the same tone of voice. 'I feel you still want me on a physical level but I also know that you have remained celibate since our break so I do not doubt your control of your physical desires. But nevertheless, you *do* want me, don't you?'

This total change of front into cool quietness puzzled her. Yesterday he had been volatile, passionate and angry. Today, at first thoughtful and reflective—and now...? Now she wasn't sure but she didn't like it and she didn't trust him an inch.

She had once, implicitly, and look where it had got her!

'I have a suggestion to make that I would like you to consider very carefully,' he continued softly. 'You know me, Leigh, you know I do not give in easily.' She smiled inwardly. The understatement of the year. 'My proposal is that you come back to live with me for three months.' Her eyes shot up to meet his but he was ready for her, his hand already raised for silence. 'This will not involve you doing anything you do not wish to do, either on a physical level or a social one. You understand?' She nodded silently, her eyes enormous in the chalk-whiteness of her face. 'If, at the end of that time, you are able to tell me coldly and dispassionately that you still want a divorce, I will make sure you get one immediately. You have my word on that.'

'And if I can't?' She forced a note of mockery into her voice to hide its trembling.

'Then you become my wife again in every sense of the word.'

'This is ridiculous.' She rose from the bench to look down at him, her hands clenched into fists at her side and her heart-shaped face fiery. 'I don't need to do this! We have been apart for five years. I can get a divorce now if I want one, with or without your consent.'

'Maybe.' He smiled coldly. 'But maybe not. We would see. But that is by the by. The real issue is that I would not be satisfied.' He stared at her proudly, his face ruthlessly arrogant. 'I need to know you mean what you say, that you are absolutely sure; only then would I leave you alone.'

It took a moment for the message in the quiet words to strike home and then hot panic clawed at her throat. 'You mean——'

'I would still . . . be around, yes.' He was talking as though blackmail—because that was what it was—was a normal everyday occurence in his life. But maybe it was? She stared at him helplessly. She didn't know him, not really. The charming companion, the socialite playboy whom she had married, was gone. She had been right. He *had* changed. She had thought the old Raoul was arrogant at times, spoilt, too used to having his own way, but the man looking up at her now was . . . dangerous. She thought back over the last two days. He had purposely set out to trap her into his bed, or, more correctly, her bed, thinking that if she committed herself that far she would go back to him without any fuss. She was sure of that now. It had all been a cold-blooded exercise on his part. But why? Why? She had no illusions about herself. She couldn't begin to compare to some of the beauties he came into contact with every day and most of them had no scruples at all. Why did he want her?

The answer, when it came, was no surprise. She discovered she had suspected it all along, even before she left him. She was a challenge. He had admitted as much himself. She did not boost his ego in the cloying way his other women did. The first time they'd met, she had been the one he was interested in, in spite of a beachful of nubile beauties being there for the taking, because *she* hadn't been interested in *him*! Or hadn't appeared to be, she corrected honestly in her mind. And a divorce would soil the family name! How dared he?

And now? What was she to do now? Could she stand him popping in and out of her life for years, tantalisingly available? The break had to be clean for her to survive.

'OK, Raoul, you win.' She saw the blink of amazement, quickly concealed, at her capitulation. 'I'll live with you for three months and only three months.' She stared at him hard. 'But you might not like it.'

'I'll like it,' he said expressionlessly.

'But when the three months is up I want your word that the divorce will be available. No hidden catches, no delay.'

'You have it.' The tone was tighter now.

'And you won't contact me again—ever.' He blinked again. 'Not ever, Raoul.'

'So be it.' His voice was a growl now—she couldn't blame him really. But she had to be strong, she had to be.

'Are you sure you want to go through with this? An agreement now would be much easier and the end result will be the same.' Her voice was flat and empty and although she didn't know where the control was coming from she was overwhelmingly grateful for it, even if she was bleeding badly inside.

'Quite sure.' His eyes were blazing.

The walk back to her flat was conducted in total silence so loud that it was deafening. There was no arm round her shoulders this time, no easy reminiscing; indeed Raoul acted as though he wasn't even aware of her presence. He didn't need her; he never had.

As they paused on the pavement outside the huge grimy building he looked down at her grimly, his hands pushed deep into his jeans pockets and his eyes almost opaque. 'I'll be in touch. Arrangements and so on.'

'OK.' There was something in her that longed to reach out and smooth the harsh lines round his mouth, and it terrified her.

'Is there anyone you need to contact? That aunt in Scotland who came to our wedding?' he asked tightly.

'She died last year.' Aunt Jess's daughter was her only living relative now and they had lost contact shortly after she had married Raoul. 'I'll take care of things anyway,' she added quietly, 'I'm used to fending for myself.'

'Yes.' The one word carried a wealth of feeling and she stared up at him, her gaze faltering at the dangerous glitter in his eyes. 'Get your passport in order. We fly to France the day after tomorrow.' His tone brooked no argument.

'Raoul——' This coldness was ripping her apart.

'You are committed now. I have your word.' His mouth had thinned and his eyes were cold but he had never looked more handsome, or more remote. He left her abruptly, striding off down the street, sure-footed as a big cat with his head held high and his broad shoulders back. She saw at least three women almost fall over themselves before he reached the corner and was lost from view, and she bit on her lower lip in hot panic. She shouldn't have agreed to this crazy scheme! It meant three months of misery and her work would suffer—she really couldn't afford to be away from London at the moment. Why hadn't she thought of that when he set out his demands? She shut her eyes tightly for a second. Because when he was around lucid thought was a commodity in very short supply!

She had barely entered the flat when the phone rang. 'I forgot to mention it.' His voice was flat and polite. 'I will pay the rent of the flat for three months in advance. Yes?'

'Oh, right ... thank you.' She paused, uncertain of how to continue, and then the phone was re-placed at the other end with a firm click. She glared at the inoffensive object ferociously. This was all so sudden, so overwhelming, so crazy, so—Raoul-like! She glanced round the little flat helplessly. It wouldn't take her long to pack! Her clothes were mainly jeans and T-shirts these days with one 'posh' affair she kept for parties and suchlike, deliberately refusing to indulge in more. She remembered the huge bonfire she had made of all her clothes and possessions before leaving Raoul's mansion that night; it had lit the sky for miles around! Right in the middle of the bowling-green-smooth lawns! He had been out, driving Marion and her husband to the airport; she never had known what had passed between them on that journey. She had left before he returned, disappearing into the night silently and leaving no trace of her whereabouts for weeks. She gave herself a mental shake. 'Enough, Leigh, enough. Get on with what you have to do.' Excursions into the past were painful.

Raoul made one more cursory phone call later that evening, detailing the arrangements in a cold precise voice, his accent clipped and sharp and his tone authoritative. She tuned her voice to his and emerged from the call almost exploding with impotent rage and frustration but also with a depth of pain that frightened her. She couldn't afford to forget all she had learnt over the last few years, couldn't afford to weaken now he was here in the flesh. He was too forceful, too persuasive.

But then, she wasn't the dependent creature she had been at eighteen, lost in love and adoration for her big handsome husband and quite unable to believe her luck in capturing him.

She was her own person now, able to run her life the way she wanted it. And yet... She couldn't stop her mind from wandering down channels she had closed off for months, years. Raoul, his eyes tender, bringing her breakfast in bed on her birthday. Raoul, hard, confident, outwardly invincible and yet with a depth of tenderness towards her that had stopped her breath at times. She continued, in fits and starts, to hold a mental conversation with herself all evening before falling into bed at midnight totally exhausted and burnt-out. She had exuded so much nervous energy through the course of the day that she expected to fall asleep at once, but as she lay there in the warm darkness, a slight breeze from the open window stroking her hot face with cool fingers, her traitorous mind continued to play tricks.

Raoul's hands on her body, his lips stroking her skin... Every contour of his hard body firm and smooth and gleaming, perfectly honed to sate the devouring need he roused in her. She twisted in her solitude as a wave of burning sensation washed over her, flinging back the covers with an angry jerk as she rose to spend yet another night at her easel.

'I'll never come back, Raoul!' As she daubed colour on to the palette she glanced round the small room slowly. She had everything she wanted right here. I *have*, she told herself fiercely. This was security, order, peace, and she was in absolute control of her own destiny whether good or bad. And it would be good. She would make sure it was. She nodded to herself resolutely. The next three months wouldn't be easy but she would face each day as it came and get through with heart and mind intact. And at the end of it she would be free, really free. Nothing could hurt her again like Raoul's betrayal and she expected nothing from him now. She had nothing to lose and everything to win.

She just had to keep reminding herself of who and what he was, that she hated him, would be mad to let her defences down for a moment, and that shouldn't be too difficult... should it?

CHAPTER FOUR

THE next day was definitely anticlimactic, a jumble of haphazard packing, last-minute arrangements, several minor panics and all coloured by a brooding sense of having walked unheedingly into a steel-jawed trap. Leigh didn't want to go to France! She didn't want to live with Raoul! She didn't want to be on the same planet as her treacherous, handsome husband, let alone in the same house! She gnawed her lower lip as her mind skimmed back and forth, seeking a way of escape, but there wasn't one. She sighed hopelessly. As always he had manipulated the situation beautifully to his own advantage.

It was late morning on the following day when the expected knock on the front door of the flat caused her heart to jump into her mouth and her big brown eyes to widen in apprehension. He was here! He hadn't changed his mind. Would she have been disappointed if he had? The thought caused her to grimace irritably at herself as she answered the next imperious rap. If she was going to survive the next three months with her brain intact, those sort of notions had to be strangled at birth.

'Bright-eyed and bushy-tailed?' He grinned disarmingly as his vivid blue gaze took in the huge battered suitcase and old holdall that contained most of her worldly wealth. 'No second thoughts?'

He'd done it on purpose, she thought testily, striven to look so shatteringly delicious deliberately in order to ruffle her. Her eyes ran slowly over the long lean body encased in black denim jeans and matching shirt. It didn't help that he always seemed quite oblivious to the devastating effect he had on the female population from nine to ninety, either. She had believed in that lack of vanity once. No more! It was a clever façade, contrived for maximum effect, like all the tender words and promises.

'Plenty of second thoughts.' She didn't answer the smile. 'Do they make any difference?' she asked wryly.

'No.' There was a glint of ice in the blue eyes now. 'And for crying out loud try to relax. If we're going to spend the next three months in a state of war at least smile occasionally. It makes this unjustified hostility a little easier to take.' The sheer unfairness had her gaping in disbelief.

'Unjustified?' She glared at him angrily. 'I don't know how you can say that when——'

'I can say it because I don't walk around with my eyes shut and my ears closed to anything that might prove me wrong,' he said calmly. '*I* am a reasonable human being, Leigh, ever ready to accept that I can make mistakes, that I am as frail as the next man.' She stared at him in amazement.

'You?' she said incredulously. 'You have never admitted to being wrong in your life, Raoul.'

'Possibly because to date I never have been,' he returned smoothly, his head tilted arrogantly and his face bland.

She was just about to explode in earnest when the small twist to his lips caught her attention. She knew that look! He was baiting her, trying to get a reaction through being outrageous. How many times in the past had he driven her to the edge of madness with ridiculously pretentious arguments that had only ended when he had finally lost control and burst into delighted laughter, often gathering her up in his arms and smothering her with kisses and laughing apologies as he petted her into submission? The fire was doused with the cold water of memories and she stood aside, waving her hand to the suitcase as she fought back the tears.

'You'd better come in. I can't even lift the thing,' she said quietly, her eyes closing against him.

'Leigh?' He took her arm as he kicked the door shut behind him, all laughter sliding from his face. 'I know you don't trust me, probably wish you'd never met me, but can't you at least try to make this work?' He moved her to arm's length and stared down into her heart-shaped face, his eyes magnetic. 'You're not giving me a chance.'

'I don't want to give you a chance,' she replied honestly, her eyes darkening as she forced her body to show no reaction to his touch. *I dare not*, her mind reiterated with screaming emphasis. I've been here before and it hurt too much.

'I don't believe you.' His eyes were burning her with their intensity. 'You belong to me, Leigh, and

I want you. No other man can make you feel the way I do. There is no escape.'

'No.' The word was very final. 'When you broke our marriage vows you broke the cord that held me to you. I don't want to go back to that life again; it's over, finished with.' His hands on her arms were scorching proof of the invalidity of the statement but she prayed he couldn't feel the trembling in the pit of her stomach that his nearness was causing. 'I don't need you any more.'

'You do not?' he said softly after a long minute had ticked by in complete silence. 'I am tempted to prove you wrong now but...' He paused menacingly. 'I can wait, kitten.' He touched her hair in its high ponytail with a small smile brushing his lips. 'You look more like the old Leigh with this horse's tail.'

'It's a ponytail,' she corrected mechanically as her heart missed a beat and then pounded madly, forcing the blood to sing in her ears. The few times his excellent English had let him down in the past had always produced an inexplicable feeling of tenderness in her and she was horrified to find that that emotion was back, its pull on her heart-strings insiduous.

'Ah, yes, the ponytail.' His eyes were serious. 'Your hair used to be so short, so... urchin-like. It is nice now.' He nodded slowly. 'You can be the old Leigh or the new Leigh, all with the change of the hairstyle.'

'The old Leigh is dead, Raoul,' she said carefully, fighting the weakness that was threatening to take her over. 'And a change of hairstyle can't bring her back. Now, shall we go?' She looked up at him defiantly, her eyes cloudy.

'Yes, we will go, my Leigh,' he agreed softly. 'But first I must ask you...this Jeff? You have contacted him? Told him I have taken you away?' The words 'from him' were as clear between them as though he had voiced them and she stared back at him for a moment before replying. She had been right, she told herself silently with an unaccountable feeling of depression washing over her. She had wounded his pride five years ago, the one woman who had actually walked out on him, the great Raoul de Chevnair. And through those long months and years she hadn't looked at another man, had refused all male overtures with an abruptness bordering on rudeness. But Jeff...Jeff had been different. Gentle, kind, unassuming... Their relationship had begun with friendship and still was on that level as far as she was concerned, but she knew that she meant more to Jeff than just a friend. He had made it clear several times in the last few months, accepting her gentle rebuffs with good humour and understanding, but with a quiet tenacity for more that had amazed her. And somehow Raoul knew. She glanced at the hard handsome face in front of her warily, her thoughts in her eyes.

'I can't say I blame him, Leigh, but there is no way he is going to lay so much as a finger on you,' Raoul said expressionlessly, the content of his words taking a few seconds to register, spoken as they were in such an emotionless voice.

'What?' She stared at him in confusion as her anger spiralled. 'You know nothing about it and it's nothing to do with you. My friends are my own business——'

'Not when they care for you in the way he does,' Raoul said tightly. 'You are *my* wife and don't forget it.'

'This is ridiculous,' she said indignantly, her warm brown eyes freezing over like the breath of winter on a summer's day. 'You know nothing about it, so please don't make assumptions you can't prove.'

'You should know me better than that.' He walked over to the massive suitcase, lifting it easily with one hand as he slung her light jacket into her arms. 'Even when you knew me I always made sure of my facts and more so in the last few years.' He faced her calmly. 'You have made that necessary.'

'What do you mean?' She stared at him resentfully. 'You don't even know him. How can you——?' She stopped abruptly. There was something deep in the glittering depths of those piercing ice-blue eyes that told her differently. 'You've been to see him?' Her voice was a squeak of fury.

'Of course,' Raoul said coolly as he walked to the door, opening it with his free hand and beckoning her forward. 'I *happened* to be in Germany in the same hotel as him last week. We had an . . . interesting conversation about the girl he had left behind in England who also happens to be my wife. He was quite frank.' There was open hostility on his face now.

'Did he know who you were?' Leigh asked faintly.

'Of course.' He glared at her sharply. 'Raoul de Chevnair does not skulk about in the shadows. I told him I had come to see him on neutral territory, as it were. I wanted to know his intentions towards you. He was not ashamed to tell me. He is a good man. In other circumstances I could have liked him.'

'You could have liked him?' Her voice was shrill with outrage. 'Raoul, I just don't believe——'

'He made it clear that he wants to marry you, Leigh, but of course you know this,' he continued calmly. 'He also indicated that you do not return his feelings, not as deeply as he would wish. That you value him as a close friend and that is all. Is this true?'

'You...' Words failed her and she spluttered into silence as he moved forward and pushed her through the door, picking up the holdall and handing it to her as he did so.

Was she mad? Was he mad? Was this all some sort of aberration, a weird kind of insanity that had her imagining he was here, with her, and had just told her that he had been to warn off the one true friend she had in all the world? But it was too compelling to be a fantasy. He *was* here and oh, how she hated him at this moment.

'What did you say to him?' She stopped dead still in the corridor, refusing to walk towards the lift, her small body stiff with outrage and her face bright pink with anger. 'Did you upset him?'

'Did I...?' He dropped the suitcase and took her in his arms before she realised what was happening and now his eyes were furiously, murderously angry. 'Did I upset him?' He stared down at her, his mouth a thin white line in the darkness of his face. 'Oh, believe me, Leigh, he got off very lightly, very lightly indeed.' He shook her slightly, causing the silky brown ponytail to bob helplessly against her neck as he swore softly in his native tongue. 'You are mine. I know it and now he knows it. You are a de Chevnair!' His mouth came down savagely on hers, devouring her lips with an angry passion that had no tenderness in its depths, a wild ravening hunger in his face that terrified her with its ferocity. Even as she started to struggle the whirring of the lift brought him back to his senses and he had released her and picked up the suitcase again before the doors opened, leaving her shaking and numb as she followed him into the small metal cage. What was she doing? What *was* she doing? She should never have agreed to this fiasco.

The drive to the small private airport where Raoul kept his plane was conducted in a tight, bitingly cold silence that crackled with tension and made her feel totally disorientated and a little light-headed. She didn't look at him and as far as she knew he didn't glance at her once during the painfully tense journey. How was she going to stand three months of this? The whole thing was crazy. He wanted her back because she was his possession, that was all, a possession that had gone astray. It was all so cruel, so unreal.

'Shall we begin again, Leigh?' He had stopped the car just before the entrance into the neat tree-enclosed airport, letting the engine purr gently as he turned to her, resting both hands on the wheel, his eyes veiled. 'This is not how I want it to be.'

'No?' She glanced at him warily. 'How exactly *do* you envisage this...trial reunion?' she asked painfully.

He stared at her for one long still moment before running a large hand through the shock of black curly hair, and leaning back into the soft leather seat with a deep sigh. 'How do I see it?' He shut his eyes as she relaxed slightly, stretching his long legs in the close confines of the car. 'It is axiomatic that once you are fairly complete in yourself, settled as your own person, you can see a relationship clearly for what it is, or isn't.' He shifted slightly, his eyes still closed against her. 'I am trusting that you have matured sufficiently to have grown into this awareness, both to see how things are now and maybe to have the courage to delve into that forbidden area you have closed off in your mind. To open locked doors, maybe to admit there were things you couldn't understand feeling as you did, things you couldn't accept then.'

'By things do I take it you mean Marion?' The name was still painful, she guessed it always would be.

'Yes.' Now the brilliant eyes opened to fix on her small face, their colour almost opaque in the bright sunlight streaming in the car. 'That is exactly what I mean. You are older now, more sure of yourself, satisfied with your potential to achieve. You can afford to be generous and open your heart again.'

And accept his other women? Oh, no! No way! As hot, painful, angry tears pricked the backs of her eyes she stared blindly at the deserted stretch of road adjoining the fenced enclosure of the airfield, the heat shimmering like a transparent veil just above the concrete surface and the tall poplar trees that bordered the fence still and statuesque in the hot June sun. 'Afford to be generous?' His words reverberated in her ears like a clanging bell. Turn a blind eye to his affairs, in other words? Accept that as she had the privilege of being his wife she should allow him his little diversions? He had never really loved her; he couldn't have, to suggest such a monstrous proposal.

'I don't accept any of what you are saying.' She strove with all her might not to let the trembling that was in her stomach come through into her words. He must never know how much he was hurting her.

'Then this is sad.' There was something in his voice she didn't understand but couldn't bring herself to look at his face. 'I was hoping you had grown sufficiently, found yourself. In becoming independent of me it would be possible for you to see me clearly for who I am. You never really did, you know.'

'I saw enough.' She wanted to scream at him, to tell him that he had thrown away something so precious, so irreplaceable, that her heart was still aching with the sheer waste of it all, but she didn't.

She sat, in a tight, wretched little huddle as she tried with all her heart to hate him and failed. She had thought she knew him so well and yet she didn't understand him at all. Their two different worlds couldn't have been more defined than at that moment.

She wished she didn't care for him, wished it all didn't matter, but it did, terribly. Whatever it took to live in a world where a casual affair was of no more importance than any other pleasant diversion she didn't have. The thought of another woman in his arms, of female lips pressed to his in heated lovemaking, sickened her. He said no more, easing the car through the narrow entrance and into the concrete-lined airfield, drawing to a halt a hundred yards or so into the enclosure, his face cool and controlled as he acknowledged the greeting of the waiting mechanic.

'Mr de Chevnair. She's all ready and waiting, sir.' The man indicated the small compact jet a few yards away. 'Beautiful machine, if I may say, sir, beautiful.'

'Isn't she?' Raoul smiled his satisfaction at the obvious enthusiasm. 'I've had her a few years but she flies so well I'm loath to change her.'

The journey was easy and problem-free and that faint sense of unreality that Raoul's excessive wealth had engendered in the past crept up on her as they prepared to land in France. What did he know about queueing for hours in the pouring rain for a bus that never came? Or eating bread and cheese for weeks in order to buy some extra paints? Or struggling to pay the rent when a commission was late? She sighed silently. Even before her mother had died when she was sixteen she had been used to surviving on very little. Her father had disappeared just after she was born and although her mother had always worked there had never seemed to be enough money for the basics, let alone the odd luxury. She sighed again. No wonder Raoul's world had been so fascinating to a shy eighteen-year-old who had never even been kissed!

Pierre, Raoul's man of all trades, was waiting for them when they landed, his small goblin-like face wrinkling into a warm smile of welcome when he saw Leigh emerge from the terminal. 'Mrs de Chevnair!' Never usually given to emotion, the small man's obvious pleasure at seeing her again was like a soft balm on Leigh's bruised mind. 'We are pleased, so pleased, that you have decided to pay us a visit, *madame*. Colette and Suzanne send their warmest wishes.'

'Thank you, Pierre.' She gave the small man a brief hug in greeting, the lack of grandeur that had so endeared her to Raoul's staff undiminished by the years. 'How is everyone?'

'Unchanged, *madame*.' Pierre smiled wryly. 'Colette is a little plumper, you understand, but otherwise...' He shrugged graphically. Colette, Pierre's wife of thirty years, had been as round as she was tall when Leigh had left. She didn't dare reflect on her weight now.

'Shall we?' Raoul appeared at her side, his face sombre and reserved, and not for the first time she reflected on the subtle change in the man she had married so many years ago. What had happened to change the carefree, debonair, flamboyantly happy Raoul into the man he was now? It couldn't have anything to do with her. She dismissed the mere idea as ridiculous. He had barely noticed when she had gone and she was sure that within days his animated, crazy lifestyle had filled the slight hole she might have left. And yet...? No! She spoke firmly to herself as she walked between the two men to the sleek long car dozing in the hot sunshine. All this carefully worked-out persuasion and sweet talk meant nothing. She couldn't begin to imagine things now when she needed her wits about her more than ever.

France was just as seductively beautiful as she remembered, the countryside full of subtle scents that transported her effortlessly back in time as the powerful car drove smoothly on its way. The heady perfume of wild lavender and thyme, red-roofed farmhouses shaded by ancient cypresses, tiny village squares where old men clustered round crumbling fountains, gesturing wildly as a lucky boule won the game, grassy plains and fertile valleys... It was all as she had left it five years ago but touched with a poignancy now that brought a lump to her throat. They had been so happy once; she had loved him so much. She glanced at Raoul, distant and grim-faced at her side, and wondered what he was thinking. Was he remembering, like her, how they had run wild through the wooded hills behind the town of Ste Maxime, bathed their hot feet in the cool waters of the Mediterranean, explored the salty marshes and lagoons of the Camargue with its untamed horses, exquisitely elegant pink flamingoes and wild ducks and swans? She couldn't bear it! She found her hands were bunched in tight fists in her lap as a shaft of pain gripped her heart. She couldn't bear three months of such subtle torture.

'Not long now.' She came out of her agony to find Raoul peering down at her, his eyes veiled and his face carefully bland. 'There have been a few changes at home since you left.' It was as though she had spent a few days in Paris shopping! 'I've had a lake put in the grounds with a few flamingoes and peacocks. I never dreamt the noise they made.' He smiled lightly. 'Such a mournful haunting cry. It was as though they understood what was happening in my mind.'

She looked at him uncertainly. 'Raoul——'

He stopped her with a wave of his hand. 'But of course, I apologise, I must not make comments like this to... irritate you? I must remain in the mould in which you have placed me: heartless husband, wicked philanderer... Is this not right?' She stared at him without speaking. 'And our marriage, Leigh? When you look back on it, does it seem heartless and cold to you? Do you not remember it as it was?'

'I don't want to remember anything,' she said flatly as she turned to look out of the window. 'I just live for today now.' She had learnt that sorrow had to be taken in small doses for one to survive.

'That is good to a degree.' He took one of her hands in his and smoothed out her fingers slowly, his touch sending tiny shivers flickering up her arm. 'But the past should be used to enrich us for the future too, otherwise we run the danger of burning ourselves out.' His eyes bored deep into her mind.

'I didn't realise you'd turned into a philosopher since I'd left,' she said faintly as she tried to extricate her hand from his firm grip. Why did she let him affect her like this?

'Maybe I too have grown up a little,' he said softly as he lifted her hand to his mouth, turning it over and kissing the tiny pulse beating helplessly at the base of her wrist, before trailing his tongue across the palm in a long, slow caress. She shuddered violently before she could hide her reaction and a small smile touched the sky-blue eyes watching her so intently. 'We couldn't run wild like children forever, could we, nice though it was?'

She felt mesmerised, drugged by his presence as he carefully placed her hand back on her lap before settling back in his seat slowly. 'Five minutes now, Leigh,' he said in his normal tone of voice, probably for Pierre's benefit in front, she thought vaguely. His reference to their past life had disturbed her more than she wanted to admit, although she couldn't have explained why. They had been two different people in a different time, she told herself firmly. It doesn't apply to me now; those times have finished, gone forever.

As the powerful car climbed the hillside the butterflies in her stomach went wild as she recognised more and more familiar landmarks, and as they passed through the small village with its arcaded town square and narrow winding streets she began to feel light-headed with anticipation. Once out in the blinding sunlight again they climbed a few more hundred yards before drawing through the huge wrought-iron gates and into the long winding drive that led to the house, quietly waiting for them in the distance.

Her breath caught in her throat as she saw it again, so familiar and yet so strange now, this place where she had been so gloriously alive once. Raoul's father had had it built some twenty years earlier, just months before he and his young wife had been killed, leaving Raoul an orphan at twelve. An elderly aunt had moved to the château until Raoul was eighteen in order for the young boy to remain in the home he loved, returning when he reached manhood to her own cottage in the French countryside, where she had remained until her death just after he had met Leigh.

The house was built in the mode of an old medieval château surrounded by whispering pines with cascades of gorgeously vivid bougainvillaea trailing across the mellow old stone and charming leaded windows to add a softness to the huge mansion that competed with the red and green creeper climbing the great walls. She could remember being spellbound the first time she had seen Raoul's home and that feeling was paramount again. It was so beautiful, so gloriously unreal. She could understand why it was Raoul's main home.

'It's missed you.' Raoul's voice was soft in her ear, and as the warmth of his clean breath brushed her throat her stomach muscles clenched in protest. Where was her pride? He might want her physically but he didn't know the meaning of the word 'love'.

As the car scrunched to a halt at the bottom of the huge, sweeping marble steps that led up to the house her attention was riveted by the pure, graceful lines of a statue standing in the place where she had so ruthlessly burnt all her ties to the house and its owner that devastating night all those years ago. It was of a woman, worked in light pale marble, the flawless contours and gentle uplifted face reflecting a quiet serenity that was humbling in its beauty. She glanced at the face again as Raoul helped her from the car. It seemed familiar somehow but maybe it was a trick of the light and she was some distance away. Whatever, it was the most exquisite work of art she had seen for a long time. She must ask Raoul about it some time. He had always enjoyed collecting beautiful objects.

Further musing was swept away as the staff descended on her in a quick rush, Colette's plump arms drawing Leigh into her ample bosom in a spontaneous hug that left her breathless and pink. 'It is so good to have you back, *madame*,' Colette said fervently as she waved her arms effusively to demonstrate her emotion. 'We have wished many times that you were here.'

'Thank you, Colette,' Leigh said weakly, painfully aware of Raoul's tall dark figure standing to one side of the little throng, his arms crossed and his face sardonic as he watched the riotous home-coming. 'Oh, Oscar...' As a huge striped bundle of fur sailed wholesale into her arms she took a step backwards in surprise even as her arms folded round Raoul's massive fluffy tabby cat, who had started to knead his paws into her chest in an ec-stasy of greeting. 'He remembers me...' She turned to Raoul with glowing eyes. 'He hasn't forgotten me, Raoul.'

'Of course not.' Raoul's voice was deep and thick and warm as he watched her hold the animal close to her. 'You rescued him, after all. He always was more your cat than mine. He moped for weeks after you left.' There was a huskiness to his voice that she didn't notice as she hugged the warm soft body close.

'Did you, Oscar?' The fat furry face was eu-phoric and the tears that were so close to the surface these days pricked at her eyes.

She had found him on one of her solitary walks a few weeks after they had married, Raoul being busy water-skiing while she explored the coastline and watched him. She had heard the piteous miaowing first, and then had been horrified to see a large plastic bag floating on the water just out of reach with something moving in its depths. She had waded out, careless of the madly expensive ex-clusive creation she was wearing, and brought it back to shore, opening it to find a tiny bedraggled kitten so young that it could hardly walk. She had signalled frantically for Raoul to come in and they had raced home at top speed to try and persuade some nourishment into the frail little body. It had taken three days and nights of hourly feeding with an eye-drop dispenser before she had felt he was sufficiently recovered to trust to anyone else, and from that time on the cat had been devoted to her, growing at an enormous rate and turning into the most gorgeous creature she had ever seen. Raoul had always insisted it was a tiger crossed with a normal tabby and, although he wasn't serious, as Oscar had continued to grow—and grow—she began to wonder if maybe there wasn't a grain of truth in his teasing. The cat liked nothing better than to accompany them everywhere on his lead, walking by their side like a well trained dog and, being twice the size of any domestic cat, creating interest and mayhem wherever they went. He was utterly stupid, hopelessly lazy and without any normal feline instincts that she could think of, but she had loved him, and he her, and now the unusual slanted blue eyes were rapturous.

'I missed you too, Oscar,' she whispered into the soft thick fur, glancing up to see a dry, mordant expression flicker across Raoul's face as he watched the pair of them.

'Oh, to be reduced to envying a cat,' he said wryly as he followed her into the house, his eyes tight on her face as he watched her drink in her first sight of the home she had shared with him before it had all gone so disastrously wrong. 'Colette has prepared a light snack for us; would you like to eat on the balcony?' he asked formally after a few moments.

She turned dazed eyes to him, Oscar still firmly entrenched in her arms, and nodded slowly. 'Yes, if you like.' Her voice was indistinct. She had dreamt so often of this house after she had left, finding herself running frantically through the high, elegant rooms when her subconscious took over the consuming need she kept under chains during daylight hours. She would always be searching desperately for a tall dark shadow that eluded her, clawing helplessly at closed doors that refused to open and banging weak feeble fists at grotesquely shaped obstacles that would appear in her way, until eventually she would wake, bathed in perspiration and shaking uncontrollably. It had been months before the nightmares started to fade but as they had become intermittent she had realised she was learning to cope again and with the knowledge had come a semblance of peace, and with the peace a kind of acceptance.

As she followed Raoul through into the huge, exquisitely furnished split-level room at the back of the house whose windows and large full-length balcony had a spectacular panoramic view over the surrounding valley and coast, she kept her eyes fixed firmly on a point in the centre of his broad back. All this poignant intensity was a little hard to take. She would have to measure it out to herself in small doses.

'I'd forgotten what a marvellous cook Colette is.' They had just finished lunch and as Leigh cleared the last of her strawberries and cream with a satisfied little sigh she leant back in her seat, fully replete. 'I've been used to beans on toast and omelettes!' She smiled at the stark contrast.

'Have you?' She looked up from her contemplation of Oscar, lying in blissful sleep sprawled across her feet like an enormous woolly rug, to find Raoul's clear blue eyes fixed tightly on her face, his expression indiscernible.

'Yes.' She laughed nervously. He looked impossibly handsome sitting there with the bright sunlight turning his hair into rich gleaming ebony and his eyes reflecting the blue sky overhead until their brillance was piercing. 'A few weeks of her cooking and I shall be piling the pounds on.' She grimaced wryly as she glanced down at her curves.

'Don't do that.' His voice was tinged with sharpness and she glanced up to see a strange expression flit across the hard face seconds before the mask slipped back into place.

'Don't do what?' she asked in surprise.

'Belittle yourself in that way.' He let his eyes run over her slowly. 'I rather like your shape.'

'Oh, yes?' She forced a cool smile to her lips as her skin flushed in outrage. That had been his line in the past! That he adored her just as she was, that he couldn't bear thin stringy blondes who ate lettuce leaves to stay slim and made everyone miserable in the process. And she had believed him! She had actually *believed* him, that was what had hurt so much. Right up to the moment she had seen Marion's slender model-girl shape sprawled out in wanton nakedness she hadn't doubted that he loved her as much as she loved him.

But she knew better now. She took a deep, steadying breath. Although his desire for her body was flattering in its way she knew she was just one chocolate in a full box of varying shapes and flavours.

'Yes.' He had been watching the range of emotions flit over her face and now his voice was lazy. 'I don't remember complaining in the past.' He curved his arm round the back of her seat as he stood up, the tantalising smell of him teasing her nostrils with its delicious odour of expensive after-shave and sun-warmed skin.

'Maybe not.' She stood up so suddenly that Oscar tipped off her feet on to his back with a plaintive miaow of protest. 'But then you wouldn't have, would you?' Not with all the supplements to your diet, she thought wretchedly.

'And why is that?' His eyes had sharpened as he pulled her round to face him.

'Well, it wasn't a case of all or nothing, was it?' she said painfully. 'I suppose I was a bit of a change from the rest.'

'Now wait just a damn minute,' he said furiously. 'I'm sick to death of the insinuations that I'm some kind of stud with only one thing on my mind for the female population in general and you in particular. What exactly do you think I am, Leigh?'

'I'm sure you don't want to hear that,' she said quietly as she forced herself not to betray the panic that had her in its grip. 'You made me come here, Raoul, and so here I am, but under protest, remember? As far as I'm concerned it was pure blackmail, and the sooner we get this farce over with, the better, if you want the truth. If you want me to leave now I'd be happy to oblige.'

'Oh, no, sweetheart,' he said slowly as his eyes became as hard as glass and his face settled into cruel taut lines. 'That's not what I want at all. I've other things in mind for you. Like it or not, you're here to stay for the duration.'

She stared at this man who had taken her youth and made her into a broken, empty shell at nineteen, who had reappeared in her life just when she was finally putting the past behind her, who fascinated and repelled her in the same breath, and swallowed hard as she compelled her face to show no fear. It had been suicide to come here! He still had the power to tear her to shreds with just a few words and a face of stone and she didn't even begin to touch that heart of steel. He was an enigma, a dangerous, cruel, heartless enigma who had so many facets to his personality that it left her giddy. She took a deep breath as she turned away, her eyes dark orbs in her chalk-white face and her legs shaking.

'So be it.' She was amazed and relieved her voice sounded so normal when her insides were melted jelly. 'It's on your own head, then, Raoul; I disclaim all responsibility.'

She stopped halfway across the room and faced him again, a rush of burning colour staining her cheeks scarlet. 'Just remember I'm not the little teenager with stars in her eyes that you knew so well, though. I've grown up since then, and this Leigh is not a toy or a bit of candyfloss to follow you adoringly and say all the right things. I've got a mind of my own now and I intend to use it. If you don't like it, then tough.'

'I don't remember you ever following me adoringly or saying all the right things,' he said wryly as a touch of something akin to amusement touched the hard mouth for a moment. 'In fact that mind of your own that you just mentioned met me head-on on more than one occasion. As for being a toy...' He grimaced his distaste at the idea. 'No one in their right mind could ever accuse you of being a toy, Leigh.'

She stared at him hard, unsure in the view of his apparent quietness after the rage of a few minutes before if he was being insulting or placatory. She couldn't read anything in the cold blue eyes to indicate his feelings. He always had had the ability to turn into an ice-man, she reflected bitterly; another of his little attributes that worked totally to his advantage.

'I'm not your wife any more, Raoul,' she said softly, her voice now as low as his. 'Not in here, not where it counts.' She touched her heart lightly.

'No?' He smiled thoughtfully, his eyes stroking over her hot face and angry eyes. 'We shall see, my sweet kitten, we shall see.'

As she left the room, the blood pounding in her ears and her limbs as cold as ice, she wondered if he had known how much strength it had taken her to lie. She was his wife, would always be his wife.

Why, she wouldn't even begin to contemplate. She just knew, with an overwhelming sadness that bordered on pain, that as usual Raoul had manipulated everything perfectly again. Jeff was a friend, nothing more, and now she had seen Raoul again she knew she was destined to live her life alone. She hadn't taken her marriage vows lightly; she would always remain his in that deep recess of her mind, and when he married again, as he was bound to, the last nut and bolt in her solitary future would slide into place.

CHAPTER FIVE

'WOULD you like to cool down with a dip in the pool?' Raoul had followed Leigh out into the massive entrance hall that was big enough to hold a party in, his voice slightly mocking and his face sanguine. For a moment the urge to go for number three and smack the arrogant assurance from his eyes was uppermost, but in the same instant she realised she was committed to three whole months in his presence. There had to be some sort of compromise, for her sake as well as his.

'That would be lovely.' She tried for light coolness and was rather pleased with the result until she saw the wicked gleam in those deadly blue eyes.

'Follow me, then, sweetheart. I will lead you to your room in case you have forgotten the way.' He smiled sardonically at the fixed smile on her lips as he passed her, placing a firm hand at her elbow as he urged her towards the huge curving staircase. She wanted to make a tart retort and ask him to remove his hand from her arm but bit back the hot words just in time. She musn't give him the satisfaction of seeing just how much he could still hurt her.

'*Madame*'s quarters.' He flung open the door in front of him and urged her through before she could draw breath, but as she stepped over the threshold she came to a halt so sharply that he cannoned into her back, both hands going round her middle as he steadied himself.

'Oh, no, Raoul, oh, no...' She pushed his hands from her waist as she spoke, turning to face him with her mouth white with panic and shock. 'If I'm not mistaken, you are still in residence in these rooms. I want my own room, understand?'

'Kitten, kitten...' He leant back against the doorpost, his eyes laughing at her outrage. 'You have always slept in these rooms; they are yours.'

'They are also yours,' she said sharply, 'and no way am I sharing your bed. I mean it, Raoul. If that is what you've got in mind you can forget it.'

'I have so many things in mind,' he drawled lazily as his eyes expertly stripped every stitch of clothing from her small frame, 'and all of them delightful.'

'Huh!' She glared at him furiously, resentful of the cool mockery. 'It takes two to tango!'

'Oh, it does,' he agreed smoothly, 'it really does. And we tangoed so beautifully, did we not?' His eyes dared her to disagree.

'"Did" is the operative word,' she said flatly 'which you would do well to keep in mind.' He looked so big and dark and compelling as he leaned nonchalantly watching her, his vivid blue eyes wicked in the tanned darkness of his face, and his hands thrust casually in his jeans pockets. He was cool and faintly sardonic and completely at his ease, but she knew from experience that his stance could change in an instant into white-hot desire that would take her with him to the heights. In the early days she had revelled in her power over this totally masculine, dangerous man who could have had any woman he wanted at the crook of his finger, but now... Now she didn't trust the message his body was sending hers so eloquently. It didn't mean anything to him, not really, beyond the knowledge that he could subjugate her, mould her to his will. He wanted her because he thought she didn't want him. That was all there was to it, and if she didn't remember that she deserved everything she would certainly get, she thought painfully. And she was nobody's fool now. No matter how tempting the enticement.

'I want my own room, Raoul,' she repeated firmly, forcing her gaze away from the dancing eyes with a faint feeling of despair. 'I mean it, or I leave now.'

'What will Colette and the others think?' he asked mildly, but the hard body had stiffened and she knew he had realised she meant what she said. 'They are delighted to see you home again and they have no idea of our... arrangement.'

'No?' She glanced at him quickly. 'Why not?'

'Because, much as I trust Colette and Pierre, they are too French to keep silent about our peculiarities in their own quarters, and Suzanne is not like her parents. She is a gossip. I have no wish for our private life to be made public throughout the whole of St Tropez. Have you?'

She stared at him steadily, her brown eyes very wide and clear. 'Our "peculiarities", as you put it, are our own business and if anyone, anyone at all,

wants to speculate on our sleeping arrangements
that's their affair. I can't control what other people
think, Raoul, and I don't intend to worry about it
either.' Her chin had risen proudly as she spoke.

He held her gaze for a long, still minute and then
smiled slowly, something in his face she couldn't
quite fathom sending goose-pimples down her
spine. 'So my kitten has really grown up,' he said
softly. 'This is good. I like the assertive independent lady you have become, my Leigh, as long
as . . .' He paused as his eyes wandered over her
watching face. 'As long as you remember that in
the final analysis you are mine.'

She flicked her head tensely. 'I belong to myself
and myself only, Raoul, and——'

'Don't make me prove what I say, Leigh. We both
know I can.' His eyes were hot now and fierce, and
something in their sapphire depths leapt out to meet
an answering call in hers even as she tried to fight
her body's betrayal. She hated him!

'Am I getting my own room?' She turned her
head away sharply as sensations only he could
arouse cascaded throughout her entire body,
shocked beyond measure at her lack of control. He
wasn't even touching her! She kept her head lowered
as she forced her features into blankness. 'Well?'
She turned to face him carefully. How would she
sustain this sexual defiance if he started to make
love to her in earnest?

'Yes, you can have your own room.' She heard
his voice with overwhelming surprise and a treach-

erous little shaft of disappointment. 'It's already waiting for you.'

'It is?' She met his sardonic gaze with blank astonishment. 'Then why——?'

'You can't blame me for trying,' he said mockingly. 'There was just the slightest chance you might have said yes, after all.'

'You pig!' she said fiercely. 'You really are the most conceited, high-handed, deceitful man I have ever met. Why I ever married you in the first place I shall never know!'

'I'd love to remind you,' he said quietly, his expression deadpan, a little twist of amusement touching his lips as she flushed violently. 'But all good things come to those who wait. I'm sure Suzanne will have unpacked by now.' The black eyebrows lifted in wry mockery as she jerked away from his light touch on her arm as he drew her across the landing to a suite of rooms opposite his.

Once alone, she found herself pacing distractedly round the small gold and blue sitting-room, stopping abruptly as she realised what a ridiculous figure she would make to anyone watching, and walking through to the luxurious bedroom beyond where, true to Raoul's words, her clothes were neatly hung away in the walk-in wardrobe and her personal toiletries placed welcomingly on the long low marble dressing-table. 'Oh, hell...' She sat down with a small plop on the vast bed as she gazed vacantly round the opulent room. What was she doing here? She needed her brains testing, she really did.

Five minutes later, clad in her thick fluffy robe and light towelling beach-shoes, she peered carefully round the door into the corridor beyond. Raoul was nowhere to be seen, for which she was supremely grateful. The few scraps of cloth that made up her gaily coloured bikini suddenly felt horribly provocative and she wished she had bought an all-in-one instead. But no one, no one, wears them out here, she argued firmly to herself as she walked down the long sweep of stairs and out through a door at the end of the hall which led down a winding walkway into the first layer of gardens.

The house was built on the edge of the wooded hillside overlooking a magnificent view, and the architect had made the most of nature's spectacular gifts, both in the design of the huge split-level house and the tiered landscaped grounds. As in days gone by, Leigh stood for a moment in the hot summer sunshine, looking over the smooth bright green lawns in which the Olympic-size swimming-pool glittered invitingly. Her eyes wandered to the mass of beautifully positioned trees and bushes, their different colours and shapes moulding into one glorious whole of breathtaking harmony, and she sighed wearily. This had been her home for eighteen wonderful months and she had missed it terribly when she had left to return to the grey, noisy hustle and bustle of London. She couldn't let herself get attached to it again! Oscar appeared at her feet as though he too was reminding her how often she had thought about him in the first stunningly painful weeks after her agonising departure, and as she glanced down at his wide blue-eyed face lifted up to her in feline adoration she warned herself to take a mental step backwards. This was just a short visit, a brief interlude in her life; it didn't mean anything. She had to fight this insiduous pull on her heart.

'You beat me to it, as they say.' Raoul's deep rich voice sounded behind her and as she swung round with a little gasp of surprise, all lucid thought departed in a rush of physical sensation to be replaced by sheer panic. Her eyes seemed to have a mind of their own and as they ran down his impressive physique, taking in the broad hair-roughened chest, lean masculine hips encased in a brief—very brief—pair of swimming-trunks and still further to the long, tanned, muscular legs, she could feel the hot colour staining her skin bright red and emerging from her ears in little whiffs of steam. 'Would you like to cool down?' There was definitely a trace of mockery in the smooth, deep voice, and as she raised her eyes painfully to his face she saw that the dark blue eyes were analysing her response to him almost cold-bloodedly. They dissected her mind, breaking down and examining her reaction as they searched her emotions for an answer to what they meant. She could almost hear that cold logical brain whirring into action. What did this physical awareness mean? he was asking himself, she thought quietly. Was it enough to bond her to him again or just a mere animal response?

'Come on.' As he took her hand she forced herself not to jerk away, not to show any feeling at all.

The water was breathtakingly cold and wonderfully silky against her hot skin, and once in its concealing depths she found herself relaxing and enjoying the sensation of her body slicing through the smoothness. She had always been a good swimmer and now she concentrated on matching Raoul's strong rhythm, keeping up with him with considerable effort but keeping up with him nevertheless.

He glanced at her for a fleeting second when they had been swimming steadily for a few minutes, his narrowed eyes approving and a wry grin twisting the firm mouth. 'Is it a race?' he asked mockingly.

'If you like.' She didn't return the smile and now he laughed softly, flicking back the black curls from his forehead with a sharp twist to his head as his eyes narrowed at the challenge.

'Come on, then.' As he increased his pace she put every ounce of energy into maintaining her speed, forcing her body through the pain barrier as she felt herself begin to tire, knowing that it was of vital importance to swim to her limit although why she couldn't have explained. They swam four lengths of the pool neck and neck and then Raoul moved slightly in front as she was compelled to slow her pace, her muscles screaming for relief.

'You're still a first-class swimmer.' As she had slowed he had matched her stride immediately, and now he helped her out of the pool with a little nod of appreciation. 'I had an unfair advantage. I can swim every day. I guess you don't visit your local pool too often?'

'No.' She stood for a moment in the hot sunshine to catch her breath as her legs trembled at the unaccustomed exercise. 'Jeff and I go on the odd Sunday but——' She stopped abruptly, realising she had spoken without thinking. 'That is——'

'You needn't go on.' His eyes had darkened as she had glanced up at his face and now he gestured to the cushioned sun loungers irritably, his voice tight. 'Lie in the sun for a while and relax. You look all-in.' He was angry, very angry—she knew the signs—and yet he was showing a control of his emotions that the old Raoul had never had. She could feel his gaze on her in a penetrating surveillance as she did as he suggested and yet he made no move to touch her, for which she was supremely grateful.

'Do you wear that thing when you swim with him?' he asked suddenly after she had been lying on the lounger with her eyes shut and her cheeks burning for a long moment. She knew his eyes had been wandering over her as she lay there but she had felt pinned to the spot by a combination of sexual embarrassment and fear, and utterly unable to move.

'What?' She sat up as she spoke, moving her rounded shoulders over her high full breasts as she clasped her knees with shaking hands. There was something in his eyes that made her stomach quiver helplessly and she took a deep calming breath before

she spoke again. 'Oh, the bikini? I bought it
specially to come here. My old all-in-one wouldn't
fit in here, would it?' She tried to laugh lightly but
the sound wouldn't leave her dry throat.

'Poor devil...' His voice was dry and sardonic
with a low, cutting edge that was almost cruel. 'You
must put him through hell.'

'I do not!' She jerked stiffly upright, her eyes
flashing with indignation and her mouth tight.
'We're friends, that's all. Friends swim together and
eat together and...' Her voice trailed away at the
heat in his eyes. 'And do lots of things together,'
she finished weakly.

'Is that so?' There was a nasty twist to his mouth
now and the hard face was harsh. 'And do you
mean to tell me that you don't realise what you
must do to him? Or do you like it?' He moved
swiftly to crouch in front of her, his eyes glittering
ruthlessly. 'Do you like keeping him on the piece
of string, dangling the goods in front of him when
all the time——?'

As her hand shot out to make contact with his
face he caught her wrist in an iron grip, his other
hand coming up to meet hers a second later. 'Oh,
no, kitten, not again,' he said softly, his jaw rigid
with some white-hot emotion. 'A third time would
be too much.' He shook her gently as he pulled her
to her feet. 'What sort of man is he anyway?' She
knew he was provoking her, being deliberately cruel,
and yet everything in her rose to the bait. 'Al-
lowing you to lead him by the nose like a castrated
bull; has he no pride in himself?' She flinched at

the crude malevolence as she struggled in his grasp. 'Does he not insist on more?'

'No, he does not!' she shouted furiously as her control finally snapped. 'He is a gentleman and he is a friend—two things that you would never understand where a woman is concerned. He would do nothing to harm me. He has always put my feelings before his own. He is——'

'A fool,' he finished quietly, a look of such deep satisfaction in his steel-blue eyes that she realised with a jolt of fury that she had given him the answer this little scene had been all about. He hadn't fully accepted that her friendship with Jeff was platonic; he had wanted to hear it confirmed with her own lips, had wanted to make sure. And she had obliged right on cue. As always.

'There are times when I really hate you, Raoul,' she said bitterly, a deep weariness slumping her shoulders even as she remained fixed in his hold.

'No, you do not,' he said softly as an emotion flashed across his face that she couldn't fathom. 'You love me. You have always loved me and will always continue to love me. If I had not believed this I would not have let you go—there are too many Jeffs out there and you are too...vulnerable. But your love for me has been like...' He paused, searching for the right phrase, and she finished the sentence for him, her voice pure acid.

'A chastity belt?'

'Leigh!' She could tell she had shocked him from the widening of those piercing eyes and for a second she felt the spring of laughter that had always been ready to gush up in his presence uppermost. He slowly murmured an admonition in his native tongue as he placed a warning finger on her lips. 'I was thinking of something altogether more beautiful,' he said quietly as his eyes darkened with amusement, 'but maybe the import is the same.'

'You're wrong, Raoul,' she said determinedly as she hung on to the thread of anger that remained. She couldn't weaken.

'I know you better than you know yourself in some respects,' he said thoughtfully as he drew her arm through his and began to walk across the warm springy grass. 'For instance, I know that your father's leaving when you were born still affects you deeply now. But you, I suspect, do not accept this. Am I right?'

'What's this, a cheap course in psychoanalysis?' she asked weakly as her heart began to thud painfully against her ribs. Whether it was his words or the feel of his near-naked body against hers as she walked close to his side she wasn't sure, but the overall sensation was acutely disturbing.

'A cheap course?' He stopped and looked down at her, his eyes silvery in the bright sunlight and his face veiled against her gaze. 'Five years of being without my wife? Hardly cheap, I think.'

'Did it matter to you?' she asked wearily. 'Really matter? I'm sure you had lots of willing company to take your mind off me.' She jerked her arm free from his as she spoke. 'And where are you taking me?'

'I want to show you the lake,' he said quietly as his remote expression didn't alter. 'And don't change the subject. You don't really trust men, do you, Leigh? Your father did damage something vital?' He took her arm again.

'Oh, for crying out loud!' She twisted her head away from that penetrating gaze. 'That's not true.' She shook her head slowly. 'It's not.' Why were they discussing her father? she thought crossly. She never allowed herself to think of him.

'Isn't it?' He moulded her further into his side as she tried to draw away, his arm like a steel band and his hard body creating the most electrifying friction against the softness of her curves as he continued sauntering, almost lazily, across the lawns and threw open a small gate to the next layer of garden. He didn't relax his hold as he led her down the rough stone steps and as they reached level ground again and she saw the small lake shimmering in the sunlight in the distance she was unable to hide the gasp of delight that was entirely natural.

'Raoul, it's gorgeous...' She glanced up at him quickly and then wished she hadn't. There was a dark heat in his eyes that told her he wasn't unaffected by her close proximity and the brief swimming-trunks did nothing to hide his arousal.

'You're gorgeous.' He drew her to a halt as they reached the edge of the lake, a small cluster of flamingoes retreating in noisy protest. 'You've no idea how I've missed you. It's been so long...' Even as he was talking he was drawing her towards the small wooden summer house built at the far edge of the lake, its spire-shaped roof and quaint arched windows faintly reminiscent of a tiny church.

'Raoul, don't...' Her voice sounded feeble even to her own ears. His body was hard and warm against hers and he had been running his fingers over her bare stomach and arms as he talked, creating little shivers of desire wherever he touched. He slid his hands from her shoulders now, down over the full curves of her breasts to the smooth contour of her thighs, his breathing harsh and loud as he smothered her face and throat in soft burning kisses that created a raging need she was powerless to hide.

She had forgotten just how adept he was in the art of love, an expert sensualist who knew just where to touch, to kiss...

'I have dreamed of having you in my arms again,' he whispered hoarsely. 'Touch me, Leigh, hold me, let me know you want me too.' His body moved against her almost savagely.

'No...' Even as she spoke her arms had snaked round his neck as her body pressed further into his hardness. Time, the present, the past, had all lost meaning. All that was real was his body locked against hers as they swayed together in the soft air, his mouth ravaging hers.

To be held like this in his arms again, to feel his desire, his need of her, it was like coming home after a long barren journey, an oasis in a bleak endless desert. She wanted to sate his need, wanted to give him the comfort of her body. Why, she couldn't begin to rationalise, dared not.

She was aware of him drawing her into the waiting summer house without taking his mouth from hers, shutting the door carefully behind them as he drew down the small golden blinds over the tiny windows, still holding her tight within his embrace as he did so and as her body trembled helplessly.

It was as he drew her down on to the soft sheepskin rug that covered the warm wooden floor that she realised her breasts were free of the bikini top, and as his lips blazed a trail of fire over her warm, glowing skin she knew she had to stop this, before her last shred of resistance was used up. She couldn't become just another of his women, different only because of a thin gold band on the third finger of her left hand. It would make a mockery of the pain, the anguish, the long cold nights when she had thought she was going mad with the pictures her mind had painted. Nothing had changed. He didn't *love* her, it was as simple as that.

'Raoul, I can't!' As she twisted away from beneath him she caught a glimpse of his face, tense, blazing with desire, and her blood ran cold. How often had she thought that desire was just for her?

Despite the intensity of his arousal he made no effort to capture her again and for a moment his harsh panting filled the small room as he fought for control. 'I want you, Leigh.' His voice was thick and alien. 'And you can't say you don't feel the same.' His glance rested for a second on her breasts, their tips taut with need, and it told her he was aware of her consuming longing. 'What's stopping us?' There was a genuine puzzlement in his voice that suddenly made the anger kick hard against her stomach.

'What's stopping us?' She could hardly believe he had to ask. Marion's image was as real as if she were there with them.

'We're married, Leigh,' he said in a flat hard tone that cut at her over-sensitised nerves like barbed wire. 'Or had you forgotten?'

'No, I haven't forgotten,' she said tensely as she pulled the discarded bikini top to her and fastened the catch with shaking hands. 'How could I forget the biggest mistake of my life?' If she hadn't been so dazed and angry she would have wondered at the dark emotion flooding his face, but at that precise moment she was fighting overwhelming humiliation and despair. She wanted to hate him, wanted to remember the callous cruelty that had torn her life apart five years ago, but to her shame and horror she knew he was right. She did want him, badly.

'You mean that?' The raw emotion apparent in his voice made her glance at him for a fleeting second but she could read nothing in the tight hard face to show her what he was really thinking. He could have been a stranger instead of her husband of nearly seven years. The thought caused a well of bitter hysteria to rise within her and she moved quickly to the door. How often had she snuggled close to that broad dark chest, slept with her head resting on his shoulder and her body curved into the small of his back? Damn him! *Damn him*!

'This is getting us nowhere, Raoul,' she said thickly, her throat tight with trembling pain. As she opened the door she paused in the doorway for a brief second, turning to look at him again, seeking she knew not what. But the face that looked back at her could give no comfort; indeed it was a devil's mask of violent anger and bitter frustrated desire, eyes glittering with an unholy fire that chilled her blood. 'It's over. You know it's over.'

CHAPTER SIX

LEIGH forced herself to walk at a sedate pace back to the house when really she wanted to run to her room and lick her wounds like a small, hurt animal. She had known something like this would happen, that a confrontation was inevitable, but hadn't expected it to be so soon or so fierce. She felt too stunned to cry, although the lump in her throat was becoming unbearable.

She felt Raoul's hand on her arm just as she reached the small walkway and jerked away as though his touch had burnt her, her eyes wild and dark with pain.

'You are going to talk to me,' he said tightly as he looked down into her white face with piercingly cold eyes. 'I don't know what the hell you are thinking but I intend to find out.'

'Leave me alone, Raoul.' She wasn't aware that she had begun to shake with reaction but as she heard him swear softly under his breath his arms came out to lift her bodily off the ground. 'Put me down!' As she twisted in his hold he glared down at her furiously, his mouth a harsh line in the darkness of his face.

'Shut up, Leigh,' he ground out slowly through clenched teeth. 'You are driving me to the very limit

97

of my patience, and in case you've forgotten, that isn't too far.'

She relaxed against his bare chest because there was really little else she could do apart from causing the sort of scene that Suzanne would take great pleasure in reporting at the very earliest opportunity, and besides, there was something piercingly, painfully sweet in feeling his hard body warm against her skin and feeling the thunder of his heart against her softness in spite of everything.

'I can walk.' Her voice was very small as they entered the house and he glanced down at her for a brief moment, his blue eyes brilliant and a small muscle working in his cheek.

'I doubt it. You looked as though you were going to pass out at my feet out there,' he said grimly as he strode into the massive hall, taking the stairs two at a time as though she weighed nothing in his arms.

When he reached her rooms he kicked open the door with a savagery that spoke of his inward turmoil, depositing her on the bed with scant ceremony, his face rigid with control. 'I suggest you have a nap before dinner,' he said flatly as he turned immediately on his heel to leave the room, freezing halfway to the door as she spoke his name, the muscles tensing in his back as he didn't turn round.

'I'm sorry, Raoul,' she said softly as the tears that had been threatening to fall for the last few minutes spilled over. 'I should never have come back here. It was a terrible mistake. I knew it and yet I let you persuade me.'

It was a full minute before he turned and the grimness of his face was at odds with something burning deep in his eyes that wrenched at her heart. 'You're the very devil of a woman,' he said roughly with a note of pure exasperation in his voice. 'I haven't had a moment's peace since the day I met you.'

He had gone before she could reply and she wouldn't have been able to anyway. She didn't understand what he had said and yet somehow, in spite of her confusion, she felt slightly comforted. She curled up into a tight little ball under the light coverlet as her tired, sore mind sought the escape of sleep. She felt tired, painfully tired with the conflicting emotions that were tearing at her, and over all there was a feeling of fear. Fear that she would succumb to his magnetic attraction once again, fear that this weakness where he was concerned would render her blind to the futility of getting involved with him, fear that she would follow her heart and not her head.

He had blazed back into her life with arrogant disregard for any feelings but his own after total silence for five years. No one else on this earth would have the sheer insolence to demand what he had demanded. And she had agreed! She twisted painfully at the thought. Why now, after all this time? Maybe the current girlfriend had become boring? She shut her eyes as the tears continued to seep slowly down her face. Or maybe he had just wanted a change from the tinsel and glitter women who littered the beaches of the South of France?

Whatever the reason he had got exactly what he wanted. Or nearly.

Her racing mind began to slow down and after a few minutes her limbs felt heavy and she drifted into a restless troubled doze with dreams that were so unbearably poignant that she was still murmuring his name as she awoke.

'Is the meal to your satisfaction?'

She looked up from the delicious *potée bretonne*, a tasty beef and vegetable dish that was one of her favourites, to find Raoul's sombre gaze fixed on her face, his eyes filled with a dark sensual light that made her pulses leap into immediate life. 'Fine, thank you,' she said stiffly. If only everything else were fine!

She had never felt so confused and bewildered and downright angry with herself in her life, she reflected miserably. And it was all his fault! She glanced at him balefully as he sat eating with every appearance of enjoyment. Certainly nothing wrong with his appetite! No qualms, no conscience.

'Aren't you hungry?' The vivid blue eyes fixed on her again, filled with censure as they glanced at her full plate. 'Colette has planned the meal around your likes and dislikes. She is going to be very upset if you don't enjoy it to the full. You understand?'

'It's just that——' She stopped abruptly. What was it? 'The day's been a little unsettling,' she finished quietly. 'So much travelling and everything.'

'Ah, yes, the everything.' The sardonic face was quite without mercy. 'You mean the swimming, the unaccustomed exercise? But that should increase your appetite, should it not?'

'Possibly,' she said tersely. He really was the most impossible man!

'A little more wine? This at least will slip down without too much effort.' He poured her a glass of Côtes de Provence, which had been their favourite in the old days, his face implacable. He was playing with her, like a cat with a mouse!

This whole thing was crazy, she thought helplessly. This was the first day, for goodness' sake! She had another twelve weeks to get through and she had already almost surrendered to him once. The thought brought hot colour to her cheeks and she lowered her head quickly, letting the heavy sweep of hair that she had worn loose for the evening cover her pink cheeks. Thank goodness she had insisted on her own rooms; at least there was somewhere she could lock herself away.

'What made you grow your hair?' he asked softly after Colette had cleared away the main course, tut-tutting at Leigh's half-full plate, and they had started on the strawberries and cherries soaked in armagnac and covered with thick fresh cream. 'It is very becoming.'

'I wanted a change,' she said shortly, her face withdrawn and her eyes veiled against him.

'A change?' He looked at her steadily. 'I thought you hated long hair. So much trouble, you used to say—you much preferred it short and problem-free.'

'I changed my mind about a lot of things when I left, Raoul.' Now she didn't try to pretend. 'I wanted to look different, to act differently, to *be* different. I didn't want anything of the old life to remind me.'

'You can only run so far, Leigh.' His eyes were curiously gentle, which somehow hurt her more than all the cool cynicism. She didn't want him to feel sorry for her! The thought made her raise her head proudly. If he was harbouring any pity in his heart that really would be the last straw.

'You misunderstand me, Raoul,' she said calmly, compelling her face to remain distant. 'I stopped running a long time ago. I am satisfied with my life now. I have my work, friends...' The handsome face darkened slightly and she knew he was thinking of Jeff. Poor Jeff who had always been there for her. 'The hair is incidental.' She didn't know why she added the last gibe but it was out before she could stop it. 'Jeff likes it this way or I suppose I would have had it cut before now.'

'How thoughtful of you.' The soft glow had gone from the blue eyes, to be replaced by cold steel, but she was glad. She could take his antagonism far better than his gentleness. She had no defence against the latter. 'I don't remember you being so considerate of *my* opinions.' There was an edge to his voice that spoke of inward rage.

'Don't you?' She smiled stiffly before lowering her spoon to the bowl of fresh fruit again. 'Well, it would seem we both have different memories of that past life. It was so long ago, after all. We're different people now.'

'So you keep telling me,' he said drily. 'Except for one thing. That, at least, is the same.'

She kept her head down determinedly. She wished she could deny this physical attraction that had proved such a snare but she couldn't.

'What's that noise?' Raoul asked suddenly after a few minutes had ticked by in silence. 'A sort of throbbing?' He glanced at her suspiciously as comprehension dawned. 'It's that damn cat, isn't it? Where is he? Under the table?'

'Oh, Raoul, leave him,' she said quickly. 'He's not being any trouble and he hasn't moved since we started eating.'

'Leigh.' The word was an admonition and warning combined. 'You know I don't allow him in the dining-room. I don't like animals around when there's food about.'

He lifted the heavy lace tablecloth and peered under the table at Oscar's rapturous face as he lay, gently purring in his sleep, stretched out over Leigh's feet like a furry guardian angel. 'Stupid animal.' As he straightened she surprised an absurdly vulnerable expression on the cold hard face before he had schooled his features into the normal sardonic mask. He had looked almost wistful. She remembered how Oscar had always crept stealthily into position in the past when the cat was sure Raoul was engrossed in his food. 'That's the first time he's pushed his luck in five years,' Raoul said shortly. 'You're a bad influence. That thing doesn't know he's a cat.' He glanced at her small face and then gave a short bark of a laugh. 'Do I take it this is the routine for the next three months?'

It was the sort of capitulation he would never have made in the past and for a moment she couldn't respond except to stare at him with big saucer eyes. 'Yes?' she asked hopefully.

'And then?' He took a deep swallow from his glass. 'You walk out on him again. No regrets? Just cut him out of your life like before?' He was asking a question concerning more than just Oscar and she was quite incapable of answering for a moment.

'I could take him back to England with me,' she said carefully. 'The quarantine——'

'Would kill him,' Raoul said flatly. 'You know how he is about being shut up.' It was true, she remembered helplessly. Whether the memory of his beginnings trapped in the plastic bag with no avenue of escape was buried deep in Oscar's subconscious she didn't know, but the big animal became demented when confined in a small space.

'Well . . .' She shrugged slowly. 'I could smuggle him in somehow.'

Raoul stared at her silently, his eyes expressing his disgust with that suggestion far more adequately than words.

They finished the meal without speaking again, the only sound in the dusk-filled room the low rhythmic drone of Oscar's purring.

'Care for a stroll before bed? Your bed and my bed, of course. Separate. "Never the twain"...' They had just finished coffee and were sitting in tense silence, and although the thought of an intimate walk in the deserted grounds redolent with the rich scents of summer under a starry dusk-filled sky filled Leigh with trepidation, she felt anything was preferable to the thoughts pounding in her head. Try as she might, her mind refused to let go of the picture of Raoul as he had been that afternoon, so male, so vitally alive.

'Yes, fine.' She slid her feet carefully from under Oscar's considerable bulk but the cat opened his slanted eyes immediately in protest, stirring himself regretfully to saunter after them as they left the room.

'You seem to know all about me and the last five years,' Leigh said after they had been walking in silence for a few minutes. He made no attempt to touch her, his hands bunched tightly in his trouser pockets as though he didn't trust himself to let them loose, and his face aloof and distant. 'What have you been doing with yourself?'

'Oh, this and that.' He smiled briefly. 'A few business ventures, nothing too outrageous.'

'Business ventures?' She looked at him in surprise. The eighteen months she had spent with him had been filled with every pleasure-seeking activity under the sun but never, ever, work of any description. 'You mean you yourself, personally?'

'Yes, that is what I mean,' he said tightly, his eyes narrowed and his face stiff. 'Is that so surprising?'

'Well, yes,' she said with more honesty than tact. 'I mean, you didn't——' She stopped abruptly. 'I never thought——'

'That I was capable of making money, only of spending it?' His mouth had thinned and there was a thread of bitterness in the dark voice. 'You never considered that maybe I had taken time out to be with you? Put my business concerns on hold, as it were?'

'No, I didn't.' She stopped and caught his arm, looking him full in the face. '*Is* that what you did, Raoul?'

'Yes.' His lip curled and his eyes were hooded against her.

'But why?' She stared at him in amazement. 'You never said.'

'Isn't it obvious?' he said mockingly. 'I couldn't bear to be parted from you for a moment.' It was said lightly and she knew he was merely teasing her, but her pulse raced into a faster tempo despite her disbelief. If only that had been true, she thought bitterly. Maybe then their marriage would at least have had a chance.

'Aren't you going to tell me?' she said quietly as they resumed walking, Oscar padding slowly behind them like an elderly dog.

'I just did.' His face was an expressionless mask, revealing nothing of what he felt. 'Tell me, Leigh,' he slanted a quick glance at her from glittering eyes, 'how do you explain this feeling between us?' His voice was very cool and remote.

She stared at his hard profile as her stomach lurched sickeningly. What did he want to hear? It couldn't be the truth. 'Physical desire,' she said flatly. 'No more, no less.'

'Ah, I see.' He sounded very foreign as he clicked his tongue thoughtfully. 'And did you come to this conclusion all by yourself or did the esteemed Jeff drop this pearl of wisdom into your receptive little mind?'

He seemed to be in the grip of some fierce emotion that was bringing out the dark side of him, a black energy emanating from the big body that was almost tangible.

'I'm not talking to you when you're like this,' she said tightly, but as she went to turn away his hand shot out to capture her wrist in a bruising grip.

'The hell you aren't.' He swung her round to face him and she saw that his eyes were glittering with silvery brilliance in the moonlight. 'I've had silence for the last five years and it's ended. When I want you to talk, you will talk.'

'Bully tactics?' she asked icily as she forced herself not to struggle in his grip. Her refusal that afternoon had obviously hit him on the raw, she thought bitterly. No doubt it was rarely that his attentions were repulsed; in fact it was probably a first!

'If you like.' He eyed her coldly. 'Whatever it takes.'

'I see.' She brought her chin up as her eyes narrowed against the cool hauteur darkening his face. 'Charming. Well, as it happens I haven't discussed our love life with Jeff, if that's what you are suggesting—or anything else about us, if it comes to that. As I said, I preferred to pretend you never happened.'

'You really are a little——' He stopped abruptly as two bright spots of dark colour burnt in his cheekbones. 'So you don't admit to an emotion that draws us together?'

'I told you,' she said angrily as he still held on to her arm. 'Sex. You mean sex.' She desperately wanted him to deny it.

'Ah, yes, I see,' he growled softly as his eyes flicked over her pale face. 'But surely that is a commodity in rich supply here?' He was baiting her, she could feel it.

'So? Let me go, then,' she said coolly, drawing on the strength and independence on which she had relied for so long, pleased that her voice had not revealed the shaking she felt inside. 'It's obviously not going to work out and I——'

'For the last time, Leigh, and I *do* mean the last time, you are here with me for the duration. It might not be what you want, it might not even be what I want but come hell or high water there is no way you are getting out of the deal. Just accept that we are stuck with each other, will you? It is only twelve weeks, after all. Hardly a lifetime.' He had drawn her to a halt and was standing looking down into her defiant face, his own impassive. 'And there will be compensations ... You can't pretend you didn't enjoy this afternoon before it came to such an unnecessary halt.'

She flushed scarlet at the reminder of her easy surrender to his passion. That was just like Raoul!

He could at least have pretended to be a gentleman and forgotten the whole episode!

'So you are really determined to go through with this travesty?' she asked stiffly as she finally managed to free her hand just as the loud mournful cry of a peacock sounded somewhere in the grounds.

His eyes had narrowed, whether at her words or the bird's haunting wail she wasn't sure. 'More than ever.' His face had closed against her and as she searched the hard features they were giving nothing away. 'I'd forgotten just how sweet the taste of you is...'

She drew back slightly, her newly sensitised emotions picking up the thickness in his voice, but this time he made no attempt to touch her, watching her through cold, tortured eyes as she stared at him, huge-eyed, a mixture of bewilderment, fear and anger at her weakness where this man was concerned turning her face white.

'I'm cold.' She shivered in spite of the thick warm air delicately scented with the perfume of a thousand flowers. 'I'm going back to the house.'

He remained as still as a statue as she backed away from him, his broad shoulders dark against the outline of the soft night sky and his hands jammed tight into his trouser pockets. She stared at him silently for a moment. She knew it was her imagination but he seemed intensely alone, and she had the overwhelmingly insane urge to move back into his arms, to succumb to everything he desired of her, to subjugate her will to his. But this was

Raoul. Bitter recollection of the past forced its icy
fingers past the poignant hunger. It would be
emotional suicide to get close to him again, to trust
him, to place her life in his hands.

She forced herself to turn and walk away, her
head held high and her back straight. She couldn't
risk subjecting herself again to the excruciating
agony she had suffered when she had left his life.
Whatever happened between them in the next few
weeks, she had to keep that tiny part of herself that
was hidden from him intact, had to make sure that
he didn't persuade her that white was black and
black was white. It was the only way she knew how
to survive and survive she must. She had come
through the worst of the fire, she had made a new
life for herself and it would have to be enough. *It
would have to be.*

CHAPTER SEVEN

THE next two weeks were a strange mixture of pain and pleasure, of discovery and affirmation of things half forgotten. Leigh found it was a delight to be in Raoul's company again, to laugh with him, to talk with him, to share his table but not his bed.

It was almost like the very early days, before they had married, but each day was pierced through with a bitter-sweet knowledge that it would have to end. And slowly, insidiously, try as she might, she found herself wanting him more and more. She had forced herself to forget the little things about him, the things no one else saw, but now they crowded in, weakening her resolve.

She glanced at him now as he lay spread out beside her on the huge car rug, eyes closed and body relaxed. If only she were immune! She sighed inwardly as she let her eyes run over the strong, tanned face softened in sleep, the ridiculously long lashes that brushed the high cheekbones and the firm sensual mouth above the square chin. She couldn't really blame other women for finding him so attractive and maybe it was asking too much of any man to remain faithful when he was offered so many enticingly packaged distractions. She smiled grimly to herself as her eyes wandered away over the rolling hills in the distance.

They had packed a picnic that morning and, after leaving the car in a suitable spot, had explored the wooded countryside behind the resort of Le Lavandou, the contrasts of sea, sky, green hills and gentle valleys immensely satisfying to the soul. She would miss all this when she left again. She faced the thought head-on. But she *would* leave. She had no choice.

'Don't you ever relax these days?' Her eyes snapped back to Raoul's face to find the piercing blue eyes watching her intently as he lay motionless, hands behind his head, the big body spread out in lazy comfort.

'Of course.' She smiled tightly. 'I'm thoroughly enjoying my holiday.' The lie quivered between them, hanging on the sleepy air like a big black spider.

'Your holiday?' He raised himself on to one elbow, raking back his hair with his hand as he frowned slowly. 'Is that what you've persuaded yourself this is?'

'Well, isn't it?' She couldn't quite meet his gaze. 'We agreed——'

'I know what we agreed!' he barked suddenly, surprising her with his abruptness. 'You've reminded me of it enough.' There was something in his voice she couldn't quite place and she stared at him uncertainly as he moved closer to her, his face expressing the struggle he was having with his emotions. The iron control won as she had known it would, and as he pulled her roughly into his arms he was the cool lover again, master of himself as

well as her. The kiss plundered her mouth, bringing
an immediate response that was impossible to hide,
and as he moved over her as she fell back on to the
rug the smell and feel of him was all-encompassing.

She would have given the world to be able to resist
him but it was hopeless; his lightest touch brought
forth an immediate and terrifying awareness that
was devastatingly toxic in its power to excite her.
To resist him would have been as impossible as
trying not to breathe.

'So sweet and so, so fierce...' He was murmuring against her throat as his hands stroked over
her shoulders, bare in the light linen sundress that
exposed the swell of her full breasts to the sun's
warm caress. He kissed her again, long and linger-
ingly, with a melting sensitivity that brought her
mouth open beneath his, searching for deeper pen-
etration. He moved on to his side with his lips still
fastened on hers, moulding her into his body as his
hands played in the dark silk of her hair, his touch
sensual and warm, and his breathing quickening as
she moved against him.

The hot sun beat on her closed eyelids and the
warm scents of summer was all around them as his
hands slowly moved down the length of her, returning after a long moment to her breasts where
they lingered in a soft caress. She wanted more,
much more, but even as the thought surfaced she
forced herself to move away. 'Could I have a glass
of wine now, please?' she asked shakily.

'You minx!' He smiled slowly, his eyes brilliant
in the clear white light. 'You know exactly what

you do to me, don't you?' He stood up and walked across to the picnic basket under the shade of a majestic cedar tree, bending down to pour two glasses of sparkling wine into elegant long-stemmed glasses. She looked at his back as he did so, the blue-black hair against the pure white of his shirt, the strong-muscled legs revealed in all their power as his trousers pulled tight over slim thighs.

Yes, she knew what she did to him! Her eyes clouded against the knowledge. She inspired in him the need to dominate, to conquer, to prove that she was the same as all the rest, ready to submit to his male beauty. The sun was a burning ball in the vivid blue sky and she shut her eyes again as she leant back against the rug, a shaft of pain making her breath catch in her throat. Why did it have to be like this? Why couldn't he have been different? Why couldn't he have loved her like she loved——? She sat up abruptly as she forced her mind away from the treacherous path it was following, refusing to acknowledge the thought that had almost materialised.

'Steady.' Raoul had just knelt down by her side to offer her the glass of wine and they almost collided. 'You're like a cat on a hot tin roof.'

'Talking of cats...' She smiled brightly. 'I didn't see Oscar this morning.'

'I think he's got himself a lady friend,' Raoul said smilingly as he gave her the glass carefully. 'It appears at least one of his instincts is intact! The last few mornings he has come home with a definite smirk on his face.'

'I see.' She was amazed how easy it was to smile when the tears were only a blink away. She didn't know why she wanted to cry, she just did, and the weakening emotion was becoming harder and harder to fight. 'That will make it easier when I leave; he may not even notice.'

'He'll notice.' There was something in his voice that brought her eyes snapping up to his face, and as she stared at him she felt herself begin to sink into that black abyss again.

'Don't look at me like that, Raoul.' Her voice was a whisper but filled with pain. 'Not when...' She stopped abruptly. She had almost said 'not when you don't mean it', but that would have revealed too much.

'Why?' he asked softly in the same tone she had used. 'I don't want you to talk of leaving, I don't want you to go, Leigh.'

'Please, Raoul.' Didn't he know that this was killing her? She turned away quickly, taking a gulp of wine to steady her voice before she spoke again. 'Don't spoil the day.'

'We have to talk some time, Leigh.' His voice was very quiet now with that steely note of determination she remembered from the past. 'There are things I need to tell you, things you couldn't have accepted before but——'

'No!' He wanted to tell her the details of his affair with Marion, she could feel it. And maybe others? She couldn't bear it, not now, not ever. 'Please, Raoul, don't.' She had no idea of the depth of pleading in her huge brown eyes but as Raoul stared into their liquid darkness she saw him take a long hard breath, his fingers closing round the stem of the wine glass until the crystal snapped suddenly in his hand, the sound a mini explosion in the deathly stillness that seemed to have taken hold of them.

'Damn!' He looked down at the broken glass in surprise.

'Raoul!' She reached across anxiously, taking his large hand in her small ones as she turned it over and flicked tiny splinters of glass off his hard brown skin. 'Are you all right?'

'I think so.' He had frozen at her touch and now as she raised her eyes to his the expression in their blue depths cut through her defences like a hot knife through butter. 'Come here.' He drew her away from the shattered remnants of glass and spilt wine on to the soft springy grass threaded with tiny daisies and buttercups. 'I like you as a ministering angel of mercy.' The deep voice was husky and warm and when his lips touched hers they were piercingly sweet. 'But then I like you any way.' The kiss went on and on as he traced the outline of her face with gentle fingers, his touch unhurried and lazy. 'You're quite delicious, you know.' His breathing had hardened and she could feel the evidence of his arousal as he lay close to her with her body fitted against his but he made no attempt to take things any further, petting her, kissing her, stroking her bare arms and throat with tiny feathery kisses until she began to feel she was on another planet where there was nothing but warm sun, the smell of fresh grass and the perfume of flowers, and . . . Raoul.

'Raoul?' She knew she was going to regret this, knew she would probably spend the rest of her life trying to get over him again, but right at this moment all that mattered was that he was her husband and she had been without him too long. 'Kiss me properly.'

'Leigh?' He had become quite still and now he lifted her chin to stare into the burning dark eyes. 'Do you know what you are saying? You're so damn sweet, I can't take much more without——'

'Kiss me.'

Now his mouth devoured hers with an intensity that left her breathless, his lips a blaze of fire on her skin as they found the places that had always brought shivers of delight in the past, and through it all she could feel the restraint he was exercising, the control he was using that was shaking his body as though in a fever.

'My darling wife . . .' She wanted him to tell her he loved her in that moment even though she knew it wasn't true, but then he was ravaging her again with his mouth, his hands working their magic on her body until she thought she would die of the need that was a physical pain.

As she arched against him, her fingers sliding over the brown hair-roughened skin and her mouth tasting his flesh, it was as though the years had dropped away and they were just Leigh and Raoul again, young and desperately in love.

In the first moment of possession he cried out with an exultation and triumph that was echoed in her mind, and then his body moved with ascending rhythm until it was over and they lay entwined in each other's arms, her face pressed against the hollow of his throat and his chin resting in the brown silk of her hair.

All was quiet now except for the twittering of the birds in the branches of the trees surrounding their remote little dell and the odd buzzing of a busy insect gathering pollen from the tiny flowers. The sun still continued to beat down on her closed eyelids, the grass was a warm blanket under their tired bodies, and for the first time in five years Leigh drifted off to sleep clasped tight in her husband's arms.

She opened her eyes from a deep dreamlessness to find Raoul propped on one elbow watching her, his eyes piercingly blue with a dark fire in their depths that brought an immediate flood of colour to her face.

'Good afternoon, Mrs de Chevnair,' he said softly as he leant forward and kissed her half-open mouth.

'Raoul!' She glanced round dazedly and he gave a soft answering chuckle.

'I should hope so. I wouldn't expect you to awaken with any other man's name on your lips.'

As she stared at him there was satisfaction evident in every line of his powerful body and she stiffened as the full realisation of what she had done swept over her in a burning wave. 'What have I done...?'

She spoke without thinking and he answered with a dry chuckle.

'What comes naturally to most married couples, I should think,' he said easily, a twist of amusement touching the corners of his firm mouth. 'Don't look so tragic, Leigh—it's legal, after all!'

The open amusement hurt like a sharp stab with a stiletto blade. He was treating it so casually, so...

'We have known each other nearly seven years,' he continued blithely, quite unaware of the affect his cheerful voice was having on her, 'and we've been married for six and a half of them. It was about time——'

She sat up with a quick jerky movement that alerted him to the fact that something was wrong and as his voice died away he looked at her white face with narrowed eyes. 'Come on, Leigh,' he said softly after a long moment. 'You know you wanted to.' He went to reach out and touch her face but she turned her head sharply, her pain making her blind to the tenderness in his eyes, which faded as he glanced at her averted head. 'Second thoughts?' he asked coldly.

Tell me you love me, she thought wildly as she sat helplessly with her thoughts running haywire. It doesn't mean what it should mean, I know that, but tell me anyway. Tell me I'm not just another pushover like the many others you've had since I left. Tell me, tell me, Raoul.

'Leigh?'

'We'd better get back,' she said stiffly as she rose in one quick movement. 'We'll be late for dinner.'

'Dinner?' There was an incredulous note in his voice that brought her eyes spinning up to his dark face and she saw that he was angry, very angry. 'So it's back to the ice-maiden approach?'

'Raoul, please.' She moved her hand wearily across her eyes as she spoke. She couldn't take much more, she really couldn't. All this was her own fault; she had no one else to blame, she had virtually seduced him after all. And all that when she knew how little she meant to him even without the past to provide proof. She had always known really, she realised with a start of surprise; deep down, buried in her subconscious had been the knowledge that it was all too good to be true. That she was ordinary, average and he was ... 'This shouldn't have happened.'

'The hell it shouldn't!' A metallic glitter was turning his eyes brilliant as he faced her and his accent was very marked, an indication of the stress he was feeling. 'You're my wife, you're mine!'

'I belong to you, you mean?' she said sharply as a little spark of anger sprang into life. 'And what about the others—Marion? She belonged to someone else, to your friend! How can you have such double standards?'

'Now look here——' As he stepped towards her, his eyes blazing, she backed away a step.

'Don't you touch me!'

'For crying out loud.' He stopped and drew a hand across his face irritably as he stared into her huge eyes. 'This is ridiculous! Farcical.'

How right you are, she thought painfully, and I'm such a fool! Such a blind stupid fool.

'You want to go back? We go back!' He gathered up the blanket and the picnic basket under one arm, careless of the fragments of glass that were scattering in all directions, and marched off in the direction of the car without another word. She hesitated, and then knelt down and gathered up the sparkling pieces of crystal until she was sure that the grass was clear before following him, her throat tight with unshed tears and her heart as heavy as stone.

He was waiting for her, leaning against the side of the car, his eyes hooded and his body relaxed. 'Give me that.' He took the glass from her and disposed of it into a bag in the back of the car without further conversation, starting the engine with a savage twist to the ignition after sliding in beside her.

'Raoul?' She glanced at his stony profile and summoned up all her courage. 'I want to go home, back to England.'

'You are home!' The words shot out with such force that she felt them like a physical blow. He cleared his throat carefully, and when he next spoke his voice was clipped and controlled. 'You are home, Leigh,' he repeated flatly, 'and this is where you are going to remain, at least for the next few weeks. Do you understand me?'

'Yes.' She breathed very deeply and tried to marshal her thoughts into order for what she had to say next. She must try and recoup her capitulation; he mustn't guess at the control he had over her. 'What happened just now doesn't mean anything. Do *you* understand *that*?' There was a blank silence at her side. 'It was just a momentary thing, a lapse.' Her voice trailed away at his continued quietness.

He was negotiating the car along the winding roads almost mechanically, sitting as though turned to stone, not a flicker of an eyelash betraying any emotion or even any hint that he could hear her. The seconds ticked by and it was as though they were frozen in a macabre tableau. 'Do you understand me, Raoul?' she asked again. 'It's just a physical thing after all.' There was a pain in her chest that was making breathing difficult and for the life of her she couldn't have said whether it was real or emotional.

'A physical lapse?' He nodded slowly. 'Yes, I see.'

She waited for more but he concentrated on his driving without speaking again as she sat huddled in the corner of her seat, her eyes blind with misery to the scenery through which they were travelling and her body feeling as cold as ice. She didn't know how she was going to get through the remaining ten weeks, seeing him every day, having him close, without being able to touch or—— She shut her mind to her thoughts with desperate firmness.

'We will be flying out to Kuana the day after tomorrow.' As his cool expressionless voice cut into her desolation her eyes shot up to his face. 'For a week or two, maybe.' Kuana. Raoul's magical little island in the sun where they had spent such an idyllic honeymoon amid tall waving palms and soft white sands. The place that was guaranteed to tug at her heartstrings invoking old memories that were best left alone.

'I don't want to go to Kuana,' she said flatly. 'You go if you want. I'll stay here.'

'You're coming.' He glanced at her angrily. 'Most women would give their eye-teeth to have a couple of weeks basking in the Caribbean! Anyone would think I was suggesting the salt mines in Siberia.'

'I don't want to go,' she repeated stubbornly. 'Our agreement said nothing about——'

'Our agreement said you would come back to live with me for three months. "Whither thou goest, I will go" and so on.' He eyed her grimly. 'What's the matter with Kuana anyway?' There was a glitter of silver in his eyes that told her he knew exactly why she didn't want to return to the enchanting little island set like a jewel in a vivid turquoise sea, that he knew she was frightened of her weakness where he was concerned, made a hundred times more powerful in the seductively sensual Caribbean atmosphere. A surge of pride drew her head up and her chin out.

'Fine, fine, if that's what you want,' she said painfully. 'I thought you had business interests here to see to, that's all.'

'Maybe I have business interests out there,' he said lightly, a glow of satisfaction lighting his face for a brief moment at her capitulation. 'It is a working island, after all.'

'You have a manager to see to all that,' she said quietly, thinking of Augustus, the huge man who ruled the tiny island with a rod of iron in Raoul's absence. 'I'm sure he——'

'Leigh!' He swore softly and fluently in his native French as he slapped his hand on the dashboard. 'I'm leaving in thirty-six hours and you are coming with me. End of discussion.'

'Right!' She answered him in the same tone, her eyes fiery, just as they arrived outside the house.

'Give me strength.' He shut his eyes for a moment in exasperation before levering his long body out of the car and moving round to open her door, his hand warm on her skin as he helped her out. 'Don't look at me like that, kitten,' he said softly as he turned her to face him, stroking back a wisp of hair from her brow with one hand, his eyes shadowed. 'I want——'

What he wanted she would never know as at that precise moment Colette called shrilly from the doorway to inform him he was wanted on the telephone. It was a long call. This was another thing that amazed her. The Raoul she had known had had neither the patience nor the ability to run the vast business interests inherited from his father. Or so she had thought. Maybe there were other things she had never known about her husband of eighteen months when she had left? The thought was disquieting and she dismissed it instantly. There was one thing, a tall golden-limbed thing, she certainly hadn't known about, she thought grimly. And there could well have been more of the same ilk.

She had made up her mind to keep Raoul well and truly at arm's length until they left for Kuana and to her surprise that was accomplished with consummate ease due to the fact that *he* seemed to be avoiding *her*. Immediately after dinner that evening he disappeared into his study with a bulging briefcase and remained there most of the next day, emerging only for meals and then sitting in austere silence most of the time. It should have pleased her but it didn't, and the fact that it didn't was an added irritation.

She desperately missed his company, the warmth of his eyes on her face, the touch of him, and the force of her emotion frightened her. Her body still ached with the thrill of his lovemaking and the nights were suddenly painfully long and cold, endlessly cold. She took a deep wavering breath as her pulse raced, her eyes dark with self-contempt. 'This won't do, Leigh, my girl,' she muttered crossly as she towelled herself dry before slipping into her old cotton nightie and sliding under the fresh crisp sheets. Raoul had bought her several sets of lingerie in the first week of her arrival but she stubbornly refused to take the transparent wafer-thin silk undies out of their boxes, glancing at the gossamer-fine nightdresses once or twice as temptation reared its head but resisting the impulse to even try one on. She didn't need silk next to her skin any more, she'd told herself firmly as she inspected the flimsy bras and panties in their exclusive packaging. Good old-fashioned cotton would do for her.

She lay in the soft warm darkness with her face burning at the thoughts that were filling her mind. Maybe he had tired of this game he was playing? Maybe the slaking of his passion yesterday afternoon had satisfied the burning desire he had had for her? Maybe he was tired of her now?

Well, that was good, wasn't it? she told herself fiercely. Exactly what she wanted!

After nearly two hours of tossing and turning, her thoughts in turmoil and her heart sore, she decided to go for a swim. Maybe half an hour of hard physical exercise would shatter the destructive cycle her mind had geared into, she thought miserably. She just couldn't understand herself any more.

She gathered up her bikini and a towel after pulling a light robe over her nightie. She could change by the pool, at this time of the night no one would be about, and somehow the urge to be out in the fresh night air was paramount. She felt hemmed in, trapped by her emotions.

The huge house was quite silent and mantled in darkness as she left her room, treading carefully down the winding stairs and out into the cool night air with a small sigh of relief. The heat of the day was still apparent in the warmth of the tiles under her feet as she ran lightly down the small walkway, and then the grass was springy and soft underfoot as she made her way to the massive swimming-pool, silent and black under the night sky.

She had just stripped off her nightie and was standing stark naked preparatory to donning her bikini when a dry male voice spoke almost under her feet, frightening the life out of her. 'I'm going to be desperately disappointed if you've done this before when I've been tucked up in my chaste little bed.'

'Raoul!' His name was a squeal of fright. 'What on earth are you doing here?'

'Isn't it obvious?' He eyed her from the dark rippling water, his expression indiscernible in the blackness. 'I couldn't sleep so I thought a few lengths would get rid of some excess... energy. I was just having a most welcome rest when a white nymph appeared out of the night and undid all the good work. Are you coming in?' There was a note in his voice that sent the blood coursing through her veins, whether in excitement or apprehension she wasn't sure.

'My bikini...' She gestured vaguely at the two scraps of cloth at her feet.

'I wouldn't bother,' he said drily. 'It seems a little unnecessary now.'

'Raoul...' She stood hesitating by the side of the pool, torn between getting dressed again and returning to the house or sliding into the cool water beside him. She decided on the latter, bending to retrieve the bikini that had slipped out of her nerveless fingers, when a sharp tug at her ankle sent her tottering over the edge to land with a squeal right on top of Raoul's head. They both disappeared under the water and she was concious of hard male arms holding her tight as she emerged gasping for breath a moment later.

'I didn't put my bikini on,' she spluttered in-anely, a movement from the big powerful torso against hers bringing abrupt realisation that she wasn't the only one without a costume.

'I know.' His voice was wickedly satisfied. 'Great, isn't it?' Any reply she might have made was lost in the pressure of his mouth against hers and as his hair-roughened chest moved seductively against the softness of her breasts she gasped with pleasure. She must stop this, now!

'I'll race you.' She drew away quickly, the silky feel of the water wonderfully cooling on her hot skin.

'Well, I can think of a more enjoyable pastime, but if you insist.'

He won, easily, waiting for her at the end of the pool with his eyes gleaming silver in the moonlight, and his big broad shoulders spread out along the side of the pool. She glanced at the bunched muscles under the smooth gleaming skin and felt a trickle of desire shiver down her spine. Why had he come back into her life like this to torment and tease her? He must know what he did to her.

'We used to do this in the old days.' His voice was soft and seductive and she blushed as she re-membered what it had always inevitably led to. 'Just the two of us in the warm water in the dark.'

'I remember.' Her voice was sharper then she had intended but she had to break the mood.

'It's as though we've never been apart.'

'Never been apart?' She stared at him for one long moment before moving over to the side of the pool and climbing out quickly, finding her discarded robe in the darkness and pulling it round her tightly with hands that shook. Never been apart? The empty years of struggling without him, the agony of the lonely nights... No doubt he had filled his quite adequately!

He had followed her and now spoke softly in her ear, his voice persuasive. 'I've missed you, Leigh. You know that.'

'I don't believe you,' she cried vehemently. 'This is all play-acting, us together, all this.' Her hands encompassed the grounds and house in a gesture which had a touch of hysteria in its depths.

'We can't pretend the last five years didn't happen, Raoul! They did. Every one of them. With no contact, no communication.'

'Then listen to me, properly, now.'

He looked quite magnificent as he stood there like a beautiful bronzed statue. The water was running in gleaming rivulets down his hair and torso, picked out in glittering detail by a shaft of moonlight that turned his eyes into pure silver. 'You never did the night——'

'No!' She shook her head wildly. 'I don't want to listen to you, Raoul. My life is all right now, I am all right. Nothing you can say will make any difference.'

'All right?' His face was grim. 'Is that the level on which you want to live the rest of your life, an existence of being *all right*? Don't you want more, Leigh? You are twenty-five, dammit, not an old lady content with a bathchair and stick. Why are you so frightened to talk to me, to listen to what I have to say? Why do you feel so threatened?'

She didn't wait to answer him, turning and running across the smooth grass as though she had wings on her feet, bursting into the house and flying up the stairs to collapse in her own room after shooting the bolt across the door with nerveless fingers.

'No.' She found she was talking to herself as she let the warm water wash away the sticky odour of chlorine from her skin under the shower. 'I can't let it all happen again.' She rubbed her skin savagely, her face upturned and her eyes closed as her mind repeated his words until she felt she would scream. She wasn't frightened to listen to him, she didn't feel threatened! There was just no point, that was all. As though it was yesterday her mind winged back to her twelfth birthday. She couldn't remember asking about her father before that—maybe she had, but she couldn't remember—but on that day, with the perversity of children, she had questioned her mother avidly for full details until she had succumbed.

The snapshot taken just before they had married had shown her mother laughing into the camera and the big, handsome—unbelievably handsome—man at her side looking down at her lovingly. She had looked at it hard but had seen nothing of herself in the tall blond Adonis whose blood ran in her veins. Her mother had told her, coldly and dispassionately, that just nine months later, when her pregnancy was first confirmed, he had run off with a barmaid from the local pub, reappearing a few weeks later, contrite and charming, only to repeat the exercise three more times before disappearing for good five weeks after her birth.

'It was only to be expected,' her mother had said expressionlessly as she had placed the faded snapshot back in her handbag. 'Everyone said it couldn't last. He was too handsome, too full of life, to be confined by the laws that governed ordinary men.' Leigh had looked hard at the lined pale face before her, seeing the wrinkles that hard work had put in place long before the years should have done, the dead expression in the dark eyes so like hers.

'No! No, he wasn't,' she had protested vehemently. 'He was your husband, my father; he should have stayed with us. I hate him!'

'Don't say that!' Her mother's voice had been sharp and with a shock of horror that had sent goose-pimples shivering down her spine Leigh had realised that she still loved him. After all this time, all these years. She still loved him. What a waste of a life. What a criminal, senseless waste, to pine after someone who was essentially shallow and worthless through the years, to turn him into a god in the illusory, illogical world of the imagination. She had stared at her mother, her eyes soft with compassion, as she had made a silent vow that never, ever, would she allow herself such a delusion. No matter how much it hurt, no matter how painful, she would face facts in her life and conquer them before they conquered her.

'And I have, Raoul,' she whispered faintly as she turned off the shower and towelled herself dry. 'I have.'

As the dazzling white beach suddenly became heavily populated at their approach, Raoul turned to her with a wry grin on his face. 'Augustus has arranged a welcoming committee.' Leigh smiled weakly but said nothing. Since arriving at Lahn airport after the ten-hour flight she had felt light-headed with anticipation, her whole being tight with tension as she walked back into a half-remembered dream of long ago. Or at least that was what it felt like.

She glanced at Raoul as he sat at the stern of the boat that was transporting them to his island. His white shorts and top showed off the dark tan beautifully, the firm-muscled flesh emphatically male. He caught her gaze and smiled again, his teeth white against the darkness of his face and his eyes such a vivid blue that they were almost blinding. They had been so happy on the day she had first come here, so much in love... She caught the errant thought and brought it severely to heel. 'Had been' didn't count any more.

They were surrounded by people as soon as they landed, the women lithe, slim and dignified, the men tall and graceful. She saw many familiar faces in the throng reaching out to greet them and as a mass of fragrant flower garlands were placed over her head their brilliance and colour caused the years to drop away. She was eighteen again, hopelessly in love with her big handsome husband who had eyes for no one else.

'Mrs Leigh.' Augustus's normally austere face was wreathed in smiles as he took her hands in his. 'It has been a long time.' They were the words Raoul had spoken—was it only three weeks ago?—when he had appeared beside her like a phantom out of the past, and somehow they brought her back to reality with a bump.

'Hello, Augustus.' She smiled warmly at her old friend. 'How is Maya?'

'She is well.' The mention of his wife's name had brought a softness to the chiselled features. 'Our fourth child was born last night and so she is not here to greet you herself.'

'Fourth?' She stared at him in astonishment. 'You have been busy, Augustus!' She had danced at the couple's wedding within a week of arriving on the island, herself a new bride, and the memory was poignant.

'Two boys and two girls.' Augustus smiled proudly. 'It is good, I think?'

'Very good.' She smiled again. 'Maya is in Teryan, I suppose? When is she expected home?' Teryan was a small town on the nearest large island that boasted a tiny, but well equipped hospital.

'No, no, Mrs Leigh.' Augustus smiled brilliantly. 'It is not necessary any more.'

'Sorry?' But further conversation was impossible as Raoul drew her up the sun-drenched beach, the shimmering turquoise sea and tall palms slowly undulating in the gentle trade winds an enchanting picture-postcard of perfection. She had loved her visit to the Caribbean six and a half years ago. The friendly colourful folk, exotic tropical scenery, incredible sunsets and starry tranquil nights were something apart in her memory, an oasis she could visit with no blemish to mar the pure recollection of a magical time.

'Shall we?' Raoul indicated the small jeep that was waiting for them on the dirt-track road at the top of the jetty, and as Augustus loaded their suitcases in the back seat Raoul helped her in and then took his place at the wheel. 'I'm sure you would like to freshen up a little after the journey,' he said politely as he started the engine. 'Yes?'

'Yes, please.' She felt hot and sticky and bewildered but in contrast Raoul was the epitome of cool casualness—and yet... She peered at him under her lashes as they bumped along the dry track. There was something? He seemed to be excited, even apprehensive about something and she couldn't begin to imagine what it was.

She waited for her first sight of the large sprawling plantation house that had been built by Raoul's grandfather over sixty years ago. She had been amazed at the standard of the building six and a half years ago—the beautifully preserved hardwood floors and massive roof under which high-ceilinged rooms were cooled with the flow of air from strategically placed openings under the pitched roof had been reminiscent of the mansions that could be found dotting the larger islands. She hadn't expected such luxury on Raoul's little island.

As the building came into view her eyes widened slightly. It was the same and yet ... different. She couldn't quite place what was different but nevertheless ... As Raoul drew to a halt at the bottom of the steps that led up to the front door she looked at him curiously. He definitely was on tenterhooks about something. 'Come on.' He took hold of her hand and pulled her out of the jeep with scant ceremony for her long white skirt. 'There is someone I want you to meet.'

As he opened the front door she remained in the doorway, her eyes turning into shining saucers of surprise. 'Raoul?' As her senses struggled to take in the row of narrow white beds in what had been the opulent luxurious lounge she turned to him with a little cry of amazement. 'What is it? What have you done?'

'Maya!' Before he even had time to reply she had seen Augustus's wife at the far end of the room, a huge basket of tropical fruit on the small table by her bed and a tiny crib to the left of her. 'Oh, Maya ...' She had reached the woman's side in an instant, her arms going out to hug the slim figure in the bed. They had been firm friends by the time she had left the island six years ago and she found she was delighted to see her again.

'Mrs Leigh.' Maya held her tightly for a few moments and then indicated the woven basket at the side of her. 'You see my little one? My little Tamal? Is she not beautiful?'

'Your baby?' Leigh gazed entranced at the tiny screwed-up face that was already showing signs of her mother's beauty. 'She's gorgeous, Maya.' She turned to Raoul, standing silently smiling behind her, and he moved to Maya's side quietly.

'How are you, Maya?' he asked gently.

By the time they left the tiny hospital, because that was what it now was, she had heard Raoul's praises sung by several different people. First Maya, thrilled to be able to stay on her island rather than have to make the tiring journey to Teryan, then the solitary nurse who took care of everything from cut fingers to new babies, then Augustus who had arrived a minute or so after them to gaze adoringly at his young wife, and lastly the two young girls who kept the place spotlessly clean.

'When?' She stared into the beautiful blue eyes with a little gesture of confusion. 'And why?'

He made no effort to start the jeep, settling back in the baking hot seat as he returned her gaze, his face deadly serious. 'When? Four years ago.' He smiled slowly. 'At least that's when the conversion started. Time means little out here so Maya's first two babies were born in Teryan. And why?' The smile died. 'Do you not know why? Surely you remember?'

She stared at him without speaking as the blazing tropical sun beat down on her uncovered head.

'You mentioned when we were here on honeymoon that it was unfortunate that there were no medical facilities on this island or the surrounding ones. That we could sweep in and sweep out but the people, and especially the children, needed something close at hand. Do you remember?' She nodded slowly, her eyes intent on his face. 'So... I decided you were right.' He held her gaze tightly. 'I should have thought of it myself years ago. There is a small bungalow in the grounds I had built for when I visit. That is now home.' He smiled at the frank amazement on her face. 'Why so surprised? I valued your opinions and ideas in the past as I do now. You said I was taking too much and giving too little to these people. You were right.'

'Raoul——' She stopped abruptly. She couldn't, dared not, believe him. She didn't understand this, any of it, but she *knew* she had only made the slightest impact on his life before. At least that was how it had seemed. 'I knew you were on edge about something,' she said, more to herself than him.

'I was looking forward to showing you the culmination of your ideas,' he said quietly as he reached behind him in the jeep and placed a large straw hat on her uncovered head. 'Have you seen the nameplate?'

'The nameplate?' she repeated stupidly, and then as he waved his hand towards the large wooden sign over the door she saw her name engraved in copperplate handwriting. 'The Leigh de Chevnair Hospital'.

'Are you pleased?' His voice was soft and low and as she nodded in dazed confusion he smiled slowly. 'Good. I wanted you to like the conversion.'

'Why didn't you tell me?' she asked helplessly.

'I wanted to see your face,' he said simply.

'You did?' She stared at him for a full minute and then wrenched her eyes from his face. 'If all you've said is true, why didn't you come after me?' It was a cry from the heart and he recognised it as such.

'Because what you said on that night you left was true to an extent.' He made no attempt to touch her, for which she was supremely thankful. 'I had smothered you with my wealth, my lifestyle, hadn't I? I had transported you into a dazzling fairyland but in the process you were losing your own identity. I had to give you time or you would have grown to hate me. You needed to find yourself, Leigh. You were such a baby and I hadn't been fair.'

She looked at him sharply. Did he mean his affair with Marion? Had there been others? Was that the next step in this heart-to-heart? She couldn't handle it if it was.

'Could we find the bungalow now, Raoul?' she asked quietly, her face expressionless. 'I've got a blinding headache and I'm exhausted.'

He remained motionless for one long moment more and then turned with a deep sigh to start the engine, driving just behind the large plantation house into a tiny side-road that had been cut into the grounds. Just a few metres down the sandy road she saw a small thatched bungalow surrounded on three sides by a hedge of hibiscus, the mass of blazing bougainvillaea trained on the wooden walls a bright contrast to the light bamboo.

Inside, the upholstered cane furniture and bright long-piled rugs on the smooth wooden floor was both welcoming and comfortable, and the two small bedrooms boasted double beds and wall-to-wall wardrobes with a dressing-table built in to make the most of the limited space. A tiny compact kitchen and equally tiny bathroom completed the interior of the delightful little house, and Leigh had to admit that if she had designed it herself it couldn't have suited her better. It was airy and light and altogether charming, and also very cosy. She glanced up as Raoul strode past her as she stood in the living-room, their suitcases in his hands. Very cosy, very intimate, very... *togetherish*? She frowned to herself. 'You have the bedroom you usually have,' she called to Raoul as she moved to stand in the doorway of the small hall from which the bedrooms led off. 'Either one will be fine for me.' There was no answer but then she hadn't expected one.

She moved back into the sitting-room, the glint of glass from a photograph on the large coffee-table catching her eye. She felt a trickle of something icy shiver down her spine as she picked their wedding photograph up. A young Leigh, radiant and sparkling in her wedding finery, and Raoul standing by her side, looking down at his bride in the adoring way her father had looked at her mother. It was all transient, life, love, everything! She replaced the picture so sharply that a tiny splinter of wood chipped off the frame. She mustn't forget that the whole reason she was here, the reason she had agreed to this three-month fiasco, she told herself bitterly, was to convince Raoul they had to part for good. And it was now more imperative then ever. Because although he could apparently pick her up and drop her at will, she, unfortunately, could not do the same!

CHAPTER EIGHT

As TIME slipped by in an idle haze of blazingly hot tropical days spent swimming in warm crystal-clear waters and exploring the coral reefs where colourful fish darted in and out in a crazy game of catch-me-if-you-can, and long lazy nights enjoying deliciously cool cocktails by moonlight under the gentle rustle of the palm trees in the night breeze, Leigh became aware she was living on borrowed time.

Raoul had made no attempt to visit her bed after her dismissive put-down on the day of arrival and most nights she lay awake for hours in the humid, sticky heat. Indeed, he seemed to be keeping himself strictly at arm's length, his face frequently donning the sardonic mask it wore so well and his conversation often enigmatic in the extreme. It made for tension, and Leigh found she was quite unable to handle the torture of having him so close but so far. She knew he wanted her, the burning hunger in his eyes when he thought she wasn't looking told her that, but he was able to suppress his desire with apparently the minimum of effort. And yet ... She knew she was living on a time-bomb. She had to face the fact that the past—Marion—needed to be brought out into the cold light of day and finally put to rest. He had made that clear in a hundred and one ways.

She glanced at him now as he lay by her side, staring down the endlessly white beach, his near-naked body stretched out with animal grace and gleaming like a well honed brown machine in the white light. She wanted him. The thought stiffened her back but there was no denying it. Right at this moment she wanted him, needed him, all the half-forgotten pleasures of his lovemaking having been brought to glorious life after that one fatal afternoon. He was powerful and handsome and infinitely dangerous and she hated her weakness but... she still wanted him. And there was something else. She had become aware, slowly but with growing certainty, that the Raoul she had once known had been but a pale reflection of the man he now was. The vast business interests that he controlled so masterfully, his care for the people of this little island, his intrinsic strength... It had probably all been there before but she hadn't noticed. Maybe he was right? Maybe she had needed to step back and grow herself before she could see him clearly for what he was?

'No!' She had spoken out loud before she realised and he turned instantly, the piercingly blue eyes narrowed in enquiry.

'No?' The smile on his lips died as he noticed the haunted expression in her eyes. 'What's wrong, Leigh?' He took one of her small hands in his own as he sat up and moved closer to her. The hard male thigh against her flesh caused a ripple of feeling that in the circumstances she could have done without.

'Nothing.' She looked into the fabulously beautiful eyes and then sighed helplessly. 'Everything! I shouldn't have come here, shouldn't have listened to you, Raoul.'

'Wrong.' His face expressed a satisfaction at her confusion that made her want to hit him. 'My island has a way of stripping off all the surface veneer and bringing one face to face with all the hidden depths, does it not? It is hard to pretend, especially to oneself, in the atmosphere of such simplicity. You needed to come here, my Leigh. You would not let me in before.'

'And you think I have now?' She raised her chin as she spoke, her eyes hostile.

'Not yet, but you want to,' he said with infuriating assurance. 'I am the only man in the world you will ever fully love.'

The sheer arrogance took her breath away for a moment and then she snatched her hand away quickly, her face flushing with furious colour.

'You cannot deny this, my Leigh,' he said calmly as he took in her confusion. 'You loved me seven years ago and you love me now. It is as simple as that.'

'Nothing is simple with us, Raoul,' she said bitterly, 'and the man I met all that time ago is not the man you are now. You have changed, and I don't know how to feel about the changes.' He was looking at her keenly and she forced herself to go on. 'You are different, I'm different. Maybe there is nothing at all left of the old Leigh and Raoul.'

'Nonsense,' he said lightly. 'You are talking nonsense because you do not wish to face the truth. We are not so very different now, merely a little older and wiser. You can see me a little more clearly now, maybe?' He bent towards her to look deep into her eyes. 'This is why you are punishing me? Because I do not fit into the mould in which you have placed me?'

'I don't know what you're talking about,' she said quietly as her mind refused to acknowledge the grain of truth in what he was saying. And he was right, she had been talking nonsense, because the one area in which he was still exactly the same was the barrier to any life they could have together.

'This is not the truth,' he said quietly, turning from her to look out over the gently rippling sea that was turning a soft shade of pink as the sun began to set and the tropical bird song denoted the end of the day. Darkness fell with an alarming swiftness here and already dusk had touched the deserted beach with inquisitive blue fingers. 'For some reason the very fact that I have followed your suggestion, made the lives of the people here better, bothers you far more than any act of unkindness would have done.' He turned to face her again and she caught her breath at the beauty of him—the strong, hard, firm body, the dangerously handsome face with its compelling eyes and proud mouth. He still fascinated her. He always would. 'Can you deny this?'

'What?' She stared at him mesmerised and then caught herself sharply. 'Oh ... yes, yes, I do deny it. I'm glad you've helped them, Raoul, of course I am.'

'Of course I am ...' He echoed her words mockingly with a slightly cruel twist to his mouth, touching her lips with a stroking finger as he outlined their fullness. 'So beautiful and so frightened.'

'Frightened?' she said quickly. 'Of you? Don't flatter yourself, Raoul.' She wondered if he could hear the lie.

'Then why have you kept yourself from me these last three weeks, kitten?' he asked in a low husky voice. 'You want me, you know you do, so why deny us both those magical glimpses of paradise?'

'I don't want you, Raoul,' she denied coldly as liquid fire sent her blood racing through her veins. 'When are you going to understand that there is nothing left between us, except maybe——?'

'This?' He had moved over her before she realised what was happening, the angry glitter in his eyes barely visible now as darkness surrounded them in a thick mantle. She knew she ought to resist and she wanted to, she did, it was just that his touch was so intoxicating, the knowledge of how he could make her feel so unbearably sweet. The tortured groan that left Raoul's lips was echoed in the depths of her heart but as she responded to him blindly, with a hunger that matched his, it felt so right. The iron-hard muscles, the broad hair-roughened chest fitted against her softness so completely that it was like the last piece in a glorious jigsaw and she was powerless against the white-hot passion he induced so easily.

'How can you talk of going away, of leaving me again?' he muttered with fierce tenderness as he drew her against his nakedness. 'I won't let you.' His mouth had taken hers once more before she could answer him and she melted under his expertise. 'Do you hear me, Leigh?' There was an element of cruelty, of desperation, in his love-making that she had never known before, as though his body was reaching out to her beyond the act itself, trying to impart some knowledge deep inside her that she would be forced to recognise. 'You want me, you cannot deny it!'

He continued to caress and kiss her, to tease and stroke until she became frantic with desire and as he felt her response it overtook the rigid control he was maintaining in a scorching flood to take them both into the heights. And afterwards, like before, he held her tight in his arms against the hard protecting wall of his body, stroking her hair gently with lazy fingers until his deep regular breathing told her he was asleep.

The soft powdery sand was warm as they lay in the scented darkness and as she shifted slightly to look up into the blue-black sky dotted with a million tiny twinkling stars like diamonds on a piece of exquisite velvet Raoul adjusted his position next to her, his head sliding on to her stomach as he murmured her name in his sleep.

Why that particular stance, after all the intimacies and shattering familiarities of lovemaking, should be the final cog in the wheel of her mind that revealed the truth she didn't know, but in that instance she knew she had never stopped loving him, not for a minute. Her love for him was as inevitable as breathing and just as unavoidable while she lived. She had been his from the first moment she had stared into those wicked gleaming blue eyes and it was ordained, if not by man then certainly by God, that she would remain his until the day she died. She knew it now. He was her destiny and there was no escape.

She remained perfectly still as her mind recalled their last conversation. It was true, she had to admit it now, that accusation that his act of magnanimity to the islanders had perturbed her. It had. She dared not believe this new Raoul was for real; it cut through all her defences and left her powerless to fight him. And she had to fight him. The knowledge brought a whiteness to her lips. She loved him far more than he would ever comprehend but she could never live with him again, never be his wife. It would give him the power he needed to break her again and she knew she would never survive another personal holocaust like the one of five years ago. When had he said that he loved her? That the others meant nothing?

She forced herself not to move as her mind relived the agony of that moment when she saw Marion in their bed. The anger, the pain, the sheer impotent fury was still with her as though it was yesterday. Maybe some women found it within themselves to utterly forgive such a betrayal—her mother obviously had—but she knew herself too well now and that greatness was not in her. What he had done once, he could do again, and she couldn't live through it.

'Leigh?' Her inward turmoil must have communicated itself to Raoul in some way even through sleep because he opened drowsy eyes to look up into her face, twisting to sit up in one fluid movement as he saw the tears running in a warm flood down her cheeks. 'Leigh, what is it?' He took her in his arms and for a moment she was content to lie there against his heartbeat, held close to the man she loved, her husband, her lover, her everything. 'What's wrong?'

As he moved her an inch or two away to look more closely into her face she shut her eyes quickly, fearful of what they might tell him. He mustn't know. He mustn't ever know.

'I don't know,' she whispered brokenly as she sank back against him again, his arms going out immediately to hug her close. 'It's just so beautiful here, so peaceful. I'm being silly.'

He accepted the explanation although she knew he guessed there was something else, and later that night, after dinner, when she asked if they could return to France he didn't press her for a reason beyond the one she told him—that she was missing Oscar, that she had a feeling something was wrong with the animal.

As they left the little island late the next morning blazing peacefully under a tropical sun, the brilliant blue waters and white sands a vivid contrast against the gaily waving islanders, she knew a moment's burning regret. Maybe she should have stayed here a little longer with Raoul in this perfect, idyllic, unreal world. It was going to be all she would have to carry her through a long, cold life without him. But no. She glanced at him as he sat cool and remote at the front of the boat. She could betray herself so easily here—the very air breathed love; it was too dangerous.

'A—how do you say—penny for them?' He had moved to sit by her, his eyes crinkled against the blinding sunlight and his body warm as he pulled her against him. 'What is going on in that oh, so delightful head, Mrs de Chevnair?'

'Nothing much.' She smiled carefully as she edged away but the piercingly intent eyes iced over and now the arm round her waist tightened like a steel band.

'I don't have an infectious disease, Leigh,' he said coldly as his mouth straightened, 'and I'm sure no one would object to a man hugging his wife in public.'

'In this case maybe the wife objects.' Her voice was light but the moment the words left her lips she knew she had made a grave mistake. He recoiled as though she had hit him, his eyes narrowing into hard blue slits and his face setting into the sardonic mask it hadn't worn since the night before.

'I really do think I've had enough of this,' he said slowly as his gaze sliced into her with a touch of acid in its depths and his arm dropped away from her body as though it repulsed him. 'Right at this moment you can thank your lucky stars that we are not alone or else I would be very tempted to treat you as you deserve.'

'Oh, yes?' In spite of his anger she was enormously thankful that the tender light had died from his eyes. She could take his rage, his fury, but that warm loving look, although she knew it wasn't for real, still had the power to reduce her insides to melted jelly. 'And how precisely do you see that?'

He settled back against the wooden seat and folded his arms slowly. 'I see you laid out across my lap, since you ask, kitten, with your delightful little posterior bare to the air and the authority of my hand. I never particularly approved of the spanking of children but I can see now it has definite advantages, if not to the child then certainly to relieve some of the irritation of the adult.' He smiled with cold satisfaction at her expression of furious outrage. 'You behave very badly sometimes, do you know that?'

Now she did find her voice and with it the pain and hurt came spilling forth. '*I* behave badly? I really don't know how you have the nerve to say that. It was you who ripped our world apart, if you remember, indulging in a cheap little affair and probably not for the first time. And you accuse me of behaving badly?' She was aware, even as she spat the words into his white face, that it was pointless, but somehow her father and Raoul had got inextricably linked in her mind and at this precise moment she couldn't have separated the two. She wanted to hurt, to wound, to destroy the magic of the last three weeks on this enchanted island and especially the treacherous, beckoning enticement of last night. It was a seductive weakness that she couldn't afford.

'I shall not even deign to answer such a ridiculous imputation,' he said coldly, 'mainly because I know that you do not mean it. You are behaving like a child, Leigh. Please control yourself.' He turned his face away in proud disapproval.

The reprimand was said without heat and with an icy disgust that doused her flame of anger in a second. What was he turning her into? She sank back against the warm wood of the boat, closing her eyes against the glare of the sun and his implacable face. She had been with him now almost five weeks and her world was in tatters. She took a long deep breath as the soft breeze cooled her hot face with its salty tang. She had broken every mental promise she had made to herself regarding him, allowed him entry both into her body and her mind, reduced herself to the type of shrew she had always held in abhorrence, and how had he reacted to all this?

She risked a slanted glance under her eyelashes at the stiff, remote figure a few feet away and saw that his face was distant and controlled, cool, withdrawn and as enigmatic as ever! She could scream! She took a few more calming breaths and when she next looked at him his eyes were tight on her face, something slumbering in their sky-blue depths that suggested he wasn't quite as composed as he would have her believe.

'Well?' he asked unemotionally. 'Care to tell me what that little scene was all about?'

'No.' She answered in the same deliberately offhand tone he had used. 'I wouldn't.'

'It wasn't meant as a request.'

'I know.' She smiled with a serenity she was far from feeling. 'And the answer is still the same.'

He looked at her for one long moment and then shook his head slowly, his voice dry. 'Women! And we are supposed to be the ruthless sex! OK, play your little game, kitten.'

As the boat continued to skim over the clear still sea she forced the panic that had gripped her heart to loosen its hold. She would fight this obsession she had for her husband and win! She nodded mentally to herself but as the lull of the boat bathed her body in heaviness she knew an intense weariness that seemed to generate from her very soul. She would battle on because she must, but oh...she felt hot tears of self-pity prick against the backs of her eyes—how she wished things could have been different.

CHAPTER NINE

'LEIGH? Are you ready?' As Raoul's voice sounded outside her bedroom door a split-second after the sharp knock she sighed at her reflection in the dressing-table mirror. She really didn't want to go to this party! Why had she agreed to go with him; he hadn't pressed her, after all? Pride. She glared at the pale-faced girl eyeing her so morosely and dabbed a touch of colour on her smooth cheeks. Pride went before a fall. She wouldn't be at all surprised if that little saying proved apt tonight.

'Leigh?'

'Coming.' She took one last look in the mirror and decided she had done the best she could. Her long silky brown hair was coiled into an elegant chignon that enhanced the wideness of her big brown eyes and brought the slender curve of her throat into prominence, and the pale mauve dress with its knee-length jacket in soft silk was both chic and stylish, the shade suiting her dark colouring to perfection. Oh, well! She sighed again. He knew he hadn't married a blonde bombshell, after all.

She completely missed the melting softness in the big brown eyes that made any man feel immediately protective, the touch of feminine vulnerability in the heart-shaped face that was subtly sensual, but as she opened the door and faced Raoul he did not.

'You look gorgeous, kitten.' There was a dark heat in the blue eyes that sent hot colour flooding into her face as though she were a teenager on her first date, and suddenly that was exactly how she felt.

'Thank you.' She didn't doubt he meant what he said. She had never been able to understand Raoul's fascination with her but she knew it was genuine. He really did think she was beautiful, although his fierce masculinity made any woman sparkle in his prescence. In the old days it had made her feel so special, so very fortunate... She shrugged the thought away and smiled brightly. 'You look pretty good yourself.'

'Pretty good' was pathetic in the extreme, she thought wryly as they walked together down the long, winding stairs. Incredibly fantastic? Unbelievably delicious? Utterly—— She schooled her mind into safer channels. No doubt there would be lots of females at the party who would be only too willing to provide the necessary adjectives. There always had been in the past. She slanted a quick glance at the big lean body, fitted beautifully into the dark dinner suit, the pale blue shirt adding to the brilliance of his eyes and the thick black hair sleeked into place for once. Yes. In this case the honey would come to the bee.

'Leigh, darling!' The huge palatial house had been ablaze with lights as they had turned the last corner in the long winding drive, and Raoul had hardly stopped the car before their hostess had come speeding down the steps towards them with more enthusiasm than aplomb.

'Janice.' As Leigh was enfolded into the other woman's bear-hug she smiled inwardly. At least Janice hadn't changed. The beautiful redhead had never bothered with the affected languidness most of their set had worn like a second skin; she had always been her fiery, impulsive self, wholly tactless and, in Leigh's eyes at least, thoroughly refreshing.

'George said you were coming but I didn't believe him,' Janice said cheerfully, and then, realising the insensitivity of her remark as she caught a glimpse of Raoul's stiff face, she covered her mouth with her hand, her eyes apologetic. 'Sorry, Leigh, Raoul...' she said quickly. 'George told me not to mention you leaving or coming back...' Her voice died away as she made things worse in her own unique fashion. 'I mean——'

'I think we know what you mean, Janice,' Raoul said smoothly as he pulled Leigh into the crook of his arm and took Janice's arm with his free hand, 'shall we say in *spite of* what you've said!'

'Oh, Janice,' Leigh leant across Raoul and touched the redhead's arm, 'I have missed you!'

'Not as much as we've missed you,' Janice said feelingly. 'You were the only one I could really talk to, Leigh, and things haven't changed much.'

'Still the same old crowd?' Leigh asked carefully. She hadn't asked Raoul if Marion would be present at this get-together but immediately George had rung a couple of nights before with the invitation it had sprung into her mind. Maybe that was why she came tonight? she thought wryly. To confront a few ghosts—or maybe witches would be a better word—from the past?

'More or less.' Janice walked with them up the huge circular steps into the house, which was humming with noise and activity. The Sance parties were always the talk of the town. 'We must have a chat later.' She touched Leigh's cheek in a quick gesture of encouragement before disappearing into the noisy throng and Leigh was touched by the warmth in the other woman's face. Then she turned to face the scene she had watched so often during her life with Raoul. The beautifully dressed, indolent women, the rich predatory men always seeking new excitement, new overt thrills; it really was just the same.

It had fascinated her at first when she had been freshly married and life was new, but even before Marion and her husband had arrived for an extended holiday while they looked for a house in the area she had tired of it all. Apart from Janice and George and a couple of more elderly couples the people were so false, so caught up in themselves, so...boring. She looked round in surprise. Yes, they were! That was the word—boring.

'Raoul, sweetiepie ...' An expertly manicured white hand with outrageously long red nails slid over Raoul's shoulder and they both turned together to see a willowy blonde in a skin-tight white dress that was slitted indecently at the sides smiling seductively straight into Raoul's bland face. 'You look good enough to eat, darling, you really do. How could you have been so mean as to stay away so long?' The hand brushed his cheek suggestively.

'It was hard, Karen.' The dry, mordant note in Raoul's voice was derisive enough to cut even through Karen's super-ego, and as the tall blonde raised carefully shaped eyebrows and pouted prettily, preparing to move to the next man, Leigh caught the flare of red under the beautifully applied make-up.

Raoul's cool snub of the blonde's rapacious hunting technique was repeated several times during the evening with different women, but Leigh was not surprised that they came back for more. She had to admit he didn't encourage their attentions by so much as the flicker of an eyelash, but perversely that seemed to add to, rather than detract from, his attraction.

She was frightened and shocked to find out how much it hurt. She wanted to be over the humiliating emotion of jealousy but somehow, tonight, that feeling was paramount. Every smile, however bland, at another woman cut into her sore heart like a knife.

Maybe it was because she could picture him here in such surroundings after she had returned to England? she asked herself silently. Maybe it was because the women were so predatory? Or maybe— her thoughts gave her mouth a wry twist—it was because she loved him too darn much!

'Care to dance?' Raoul's arm snaked round her waist as he carefully manipulated her out of the group she had been talking with and steered her across to the open windows leading on to the lawns outside where a small band was playing a slow dreamy number. As the warm night air, scented with the perfume of roses and lit with hundreds of tiny swinging lanterns dotted in among the trees and bushes, surrounded them with its tantalising fragrance, Raoul pulled her into his arms, his head resting on the top of her head as he held her close. 'You didn't look as though you were enjoying yourself much in there, kitten,' he said quietly.

She couldn't reply. The old magic of being held close to his heartbeat like this while they danced easily together was too intoxicating. 'Leigh?' His voice was persistent. 'We don't have to stay, you know. We can leave right now. These affairs are all the same and it's pleased Janice and George that we made the effort. I think the sacrifice has been understood and appreciated.'

'You sound as though you don't enjoy these things either,' she said derisively, annoyed that he could read her disenchantment with the whole scene so easily and hoping he hadn't guessed the main reason for it. With all these females falling over backwards to provide a heavy dose of laudatory flattery, he didn't need her to boost his ego still more.

'You think I do?' He pushed her away slightly and looked deep into her eyes as they danced.

'Well, don't you?' She couldn't hide the accusing note in her voice no matter how she tried.

'Not particularly,' he said slowly. 'I don't think I ever have, really. An affair like this is OK occasionally to keep abreast of the news and work a few business deals, but I don't think I've ever been a party animal.'

'You?' She forgot to dance in her outrage and winced as Raoul inadvertently stepped on her toe. 'Raoul, you love this sort of thing, you know you do.' She glared at him angrily. 'In the old days we were at something like this every few days and——'

'That was for you, Leigh.' It was said so coldly, so dispassionately, that for a moment the sheer absurdity of his statement didn't reach home, and then as comprehension dawned she drew back in amazement.

'Oh, come on, now.' It was so incredible, so laughable, that she stared into his stiff face to see if he was joking. But no. The ice-blue eyes were arctic with some emotion that definitely wasn't funny. 'You surely don't expect me to believe that, do you?'

'Frankly, Leigh, I don't think I care what you *do* believe,' he said softly as he looked down at her, injured pride narrowing his eyes and straightening his mouth into a thin line. 'I thought, I really did believe, that after all this time you would be mature enough to see things from my point of view or at least to be open enough to give it a try. But you have closed that little mind off totally, haven't you, where I am concerned? How do you think I felt when we first met? Here she was, the woman I had waited for all my life, young and painfully innocent. I wanted to give you the world, show you all the things you had missed so far. Maybe I shouldn't have devoted myself so exclusively to you; I certainly paid the price for that little mistake!'

'Raoul!' They weren't even pretending to dance now and as Raoul became aware of the interested glances from those couples in their immediate vicinity he drew her over to a secluded spot and sat her down on a chair, drawing another close for himself. 'Raoul, I don't understand what——'

'Shut up, Leigh.' It was said with such savagery that she found herself shutting her mouth with a little snap as he sat down beside her, his long legs stretched either side of her chair and his hands resting on the arms. 'I thought you knew me, thought you knew how much I cared, but after that little scenario with Marion——' As her hand went out to strike him he caught it and brought it down with a little bang on to the arm of the chair, his eyes brilliant with rage. 'Listen to me! I've listened to all your insults over the last few weeks; now you just listen to me, woman! After that... incident I realised I had been wrapping you up in cotton wool, keeping you with me so closely that I was stunting you, stopping you from growing. I hadn't given you any room to form your own ideas, to trust yourself as a person, to make your own decisions about people and life. And you needed to find your own self-worth, especially after your father leaving the way he did and your life with your mother.'

'I won't listen to this——'

'Yes, you damn well will.' Now both hands gripped her arms so tightly that she knew she would have bruises in the morning. 'So I let you go, for a time—because I knew our love was strong enough to see us through until you had it all worked out. But you never did, did you?' He stared at her, his eyes bleak with a misery that was reflected in her own face. 'When you left our home that night everything regarding us went on hold, didn't it? You didn't try to think about it all, to ask yourself if you were wrong, to allow a shred of doubt to begin to work——'

'Of course I thought about us,' she spat furiously; 'for weeks on end I did nothing else until I thought I'd go mad! I couldn't believe you could let me down like that, in our own home, destroy everything...' Her voice trailed away on a little sob, and he groaned deep in his throat.

'Why didn't you let me tell you about it, explain?' he asked huskily.

'Because there was nothing *to* explain,' she said bitterly as she raised swimming eyes to stare into the handsome dark face so close to hers. 'You probably think that if I really love you I should be able to take an affair in my stride, to shrug it away, but I can't.' She twisted her hands free and stared up at him wildly. 'I can't.'

'No, I don't think that,' he said slowly as he leant back in his chair with a small sigh. 'If you ever slept with another man I would kill him.' It was said with chilling matter-of-factness.

'How can you say that when——?'

'When what?' he interrupted her fiercely. 'I have done nothing of which I am ashamed, either during the eighteen months we were together or since.'

'You——' Words failed her as she glared into his flashing eyes. 'I'm not listening to any more of this!'

She had sprung up before he realised her intentions, backing away from him in one deft movement and ignoring his low command to stay as she swung round on her heels in a cloud of silk and almost ran back into the house, not stopping for breath until she reached the huge downstairs powder-room, which was mercifully empty. She sank down on to one of the small upholstered stools and rested her hot head against the cool glass of an ornate mirror, unable to believe the suddenness of the confrontation. How could he say he wasn't ashamed of betraying her? How long she sat there she didn't know, but as her mind began to repeat their conversation, dissecting Raoul's words almost clinically, she knew she had made a mistake in leaving so abruptly. It was time they talked it out, however painful the result might be. If she left—*when* she left, she corrected herself firmly—it had to be knowing all the facts. It was the only way she could ever really begin to live again.

She raised her head as two exquisitely dressed women entered in a cloud of perfume, their hard, painted eyes assessing her immediately and then dismissing her as unimportant. As she fixed a few strands of hair that had floated loose and dabbed cold water on to her wrists, hoping its chill would calm her racing heartbeat, she listened idly to their loud conversation.

'But darling, I was *so* surprised to see him here tonight,' one gushed silkily. 'I mean, he's virtually a recluse these days, and so altogether gorgeous. It gave me such a shock. It's such a waste, isn't it, to live alone when he could give all that to some lucky woman?' They giggled throatily and then the smaller of the two women pressed closer to the other one, her voice conspiratorial.

'Is he with anyone, Anna?'

'I've no idea, darling.' The hard blue eyes were curious. 'Why? Are you thinking of making a play for him yourself?'

'Anna...' The other woman pushed her companion's arm but the high voice lacked conviction. 'Of course not. I'm a married woman, for goodness' sake.'

'That's never stopped you before.' The Anna woman laughed spitefully. 'But you'd stand no chance, darling, so forget it. He's had women throwing themselves at him for years but no one gets near. Apparently he was married once and it didn't work out and he's pining for his lost love. Terribly romantic, isn't it?' They both breathed dreamily and loudly. 'Ronald is quite convinced it's all a ploy to get the ladies fighting to get into his bed and I must say it works, but to our knowledge there has never been a breath of scandal. Oh, well...' Anna turned away to paint her lips. 'His ex must have been crazy, that's all I can say.'

'Too true,' the other women whispered in heartfelt tones. 'To say goodbye to Raoul de Chevnair...'

Leigh sat transfixed as they finished repairing their make-up and then departed without so much as a glance in her direction. 'Raoul?' She found she had said his name out loud and put her hands to her mouth as she stared at her white reflection in the mirror. Help me, someone, she breathed silently, feeling as though she were drowning as she sat there in the quiet perfumed room. She had never felt so confused and frightened in her life. Had she made a mistake five years ago? A colossal, over-whelmingly monstrous mistake?

'No.' Her voice was loud in the stillness. 'I *know* what I saw.' She dabbed some colour on to her pale cheeks. Maybe he had been discreet since then—she really couldn't believe he had been celibate—but *that* night she had seen him with her own eyes. But what exactly had she seen? The eyes staring back at her out of the misty glass forced her to take stock. She had seen Marion on the bed and Raoul coming out of the bathroom. They had both been naked. That was what she had *seen*. She ran her hand over her lips and found it was shaking slightly. She couldn't stay here another minute. If Raoul didn't want to leave she would call a taxi.

As she joined the main party in the huge lounge that was as big as any ballroom most people were dancing to the small band that had transferred in-doors as the chill of the night had deepened. She spotted Raoul's dark head towering over most of the other men present immediately and noted that even from this distance, with the crowd separating them, he was wearing that cool, wry and very remote expression she recognised instantly from in-cidents in the past. Even as she watched she knew what would happen next. He smoothly, and very determinedly, removed the pair of clinging female arms that had snaked up round his neck, altering his position in such a way that the average casual observer would have noticed nothing. But Leigh noticed and with it came a whole host of memories she had doggedly shut out of her mind for years with resolute single-mindedness. Raoul had extricated himself from countless such episodes with silent cool aplomb; in fact the night before she had found Marion and Raoul together he had rebuffed the sexy blonde in exactly the same manner at a party in this very house.

After she had found them together she had assumed his actions had been premeditated, a smokescreen. But perhaps, just perhaps——?

As she stared across the haze of colour and noise Raoul turned as though sensing her scrutiny, and as their eyes met and she signalled with her head towards the door he nodded slowly without smiling. He was furious with her, she reflected miserably. It was there in the chilled coldness of his eyes and the cruel set of his mouth.

'I'd like to go home, Raoul.' As he reached her side she looked up into his sombre face with a little gesture of appeal. 'You don't have to come of course, if you'd rather stay——'

'Don't be ridiculous.' She opened her mouth to repeat her words but the ferocity in his face stopped her. 'Wait here,' he said coldly. 'I'll tell Janice we're leaving.'

As she watched him stride back into the laughing throng, his big body taut and tight and his head high, she sensed, in some indefinable way, that he had come to a decision tonight. What it was she didn't know, but instinctively she guessed her last refusal to listen to him had been the proverbial straw that had broken this particular's camel's back. They had reached a stalemate. As she watched him return to her, his face set in granite, she knew that the next move was up to her.

Of course she could leave it, play safe, return to England and forget she had ever been married. She shook her head mentally at the absurdity of the thought. Or she could resurrect all the old pain and blinding desolation by asking him about Marion; she just didn't know if she could handle what she might hear.

Have you really got anything to lose, Leigh? she asked herself silently a few minutes later as they sped smoothly through the dark night. Nothing he could say could be worse than the pictures her mind had painted in those first agonised weeks after she had left.

She took a long deep breath and felt the heat of what she was about to ask sting her face. 'Raoul?' The grim profile was not encouraging. 'What exactly happened that night with Marion?'

A slight swerve and his sudden intake of breath were the only confirmation that he had heard her, his hands remained fixed on the wheel and his eyes didn't falter from the winding road ahead. 'Why now?' he asked gruffly after a long minute had ticked by. 'I've been trying to tell you for weeks. Why now?'

'I don't know.' She turned to face him. 'Do you still want to explain?' This close, she could smell the scent of his skin, the familiar intoxicatingly male combination of aftershave and clean tanned flesh. He didn't reply for a moment and a mixture of fear and desperation kicked joltingly at her stomach. If she didn't hear it now she would never be strong enough again.

'Yes, I want to explain, Leigh,' he said softly, his voice faintly self-derisory. 'I've been waiting five years to do just that, after all. I didn't sleep with Marion. I didn't invite her to our room. I had no idea she was there until I left the bathroom, in fact you saw her before I did. *That* is the truth. Now it is up to you what you do with it.'

It took several seconds for his cool, almost un-emotional words to sink in and, when they did, Leigh felt her body slump into a kind of vacuum. That explanation had been the last thing she was expecting, but his voice had carried an unmistakable ring of honesty. Unmistakable? She bit on her bottom lip until it hurt. Careful, girl, careful. Don't just believe what you want to believe. Her stomach was churning so badly that she felt sick. 'And after I'd gone?'

'Directly after you had rushed into the grounds I packed Marion off to her rooms after explaining the circumstances to Paul. It was the end of a beautiful friendship. Needless to say, he blamed me totally. I had apparently seduced his wife.' The harsh laugh he gave bit into the air like caustic acid. 'I drove them to the airport and when I got back it was your English Guy Fawkes. I searched for you for two days and nights without stopping.'

'Oh, Raoul...' Her voice, faint though it was, caused him to shoot her a glance of wry pain. 'Was I the business that brought you to England six weeks ago, Raoul?'

'Of course.' The car was climbing the winding route home now but she scarcely noticed her surroundings. 'I had left you as long as I dared. This

Jeff!' He flicked his fingers derisively in snapping anger. 'He needed to be put in his place.'

The arrogance didn't irritate her as it usually did and she felt a swift stab of apology in her heart to Jeff. 'Why did you wait so long if all that you've said is the truth, Raoul?' she asked softly. 'If you knew where I was, why didn't you come before?'

'I've told you,' he said quietly. 'Do you remember what you said to me the night you left, Leigh? Just after you had struck me?' He fingered his face reflectively.

'No,' she admitted, her voice trembling a little in spite of her efforts to master it. 'I can't remember much after I had seen you with Marion, not until I lit the bonfire, that is.'

'You said I'd kept you like a little pet, that you were my doll, my plaything,' he said bitterly.

'I was hurt, Raoul——' He cut off her protesting voice with a sharp inclination of his head.

'But you meant it nevertheless, my Leigh,' he said tightly. 'You said you were capable of becoming a great artist, that you needed purpose in your life, that you couldn't live as my shadow, that you were worth ten of the beautiful people like Marion.'

'Did I?' His words stirred a vague recollection. 'Did I really say all that?' In spite of the gravity of the situation she couldn't help a small dart of pleasure that the nineteen-year-old Leigh hadn't been as pathetic as her memory had told her.

'And so I gave you your time, my love.' There was a dark throb in the words that caused her heart to miss a beat and as they drew into the winding drive she felt raw panic grip her throat. Did she believe him? She wanted to, oh, how she wanted to.

As he stopped the car in a sweeping arc he turned to her even before the engine died. 'There has never been anyone else but you from the moment we met,' he said thickly. 'You have filled all my days and all my nights, even after you had gone. There has never been room for anyone else either in my heart or my bed, my little English kitten. I love you, Leigh. Do you not understand? You are the very air I breathe.'

'Don't, Raoul...' She couldn't think, couldn't function when he was looking at her like that, his handsome face ablaze with hot desire and his voice deep with warm passion.

'Do you believe me?' he asked huskily.

'I want to.' She stared at the beloved face so close to hers. 'But I just don't know...'

'Then let me show you, my love.' His lips moved over her face in tiny feather-light kisses that made her mouth open instinctively to receive his. As his hands slid up her arms to urge her against him she felt a slow growing heat begin to shiver along her limbs, an excitement that only Raoul was able to generate. They hadn't made love since that night on the island and her body was aching for the familiar caresses.

'Come on.' He cut short her faint protest by the simple expedient of pulling her out of the car, wrapping his arms around her as they walked into the house and carrying her straight up to their old rooms which he still occupied. She was shivering uncontrollably by the time they reached the bed with a mixture of confused longing, painful exhilaration and an overriding bewilderment that was making her light-headed. He seemed to understand her fears, a deep gentleness about him that reassured even as it thrilled.

'You are my love, my only love . . .' His voice was soft against her skin and as he undressed her, slowly and tenderly, it was almost as though they were newly married and coming together for the first time. 'You are beautiful, so beautiful . . .' As he laid her back on the softness of the vast bed his eyes were drinking their fill of her, and as he divested himself of his clothes to stand before her in all his maleness she closed her eyes for a moment against the beauty of him. It still filled her with wonder that this man, this handsome, strong, altogether powerful man, should want her.

As he joined her on the bed his mouth searched for her lips, his long body pressed against the length of hers, and she wrapped her arms round his neck, exulting in his dominance. Her fingers slid into the dark thickness of his hair, crisp and vital, and as he felt her hands move down to clasp his back he groaned deep in his throat, his lips trailing fire over her face, her throat and still lower to her soft body spread out beneath him until she shivered with pleasure.

'I want to care for you, to protect you, to love you for the rest of our lives, my love,' he muttered into the soft silk of her hair. 'My hunger for you consumes me. How could you think I would ever do anything to hurt you? I adore you, my sweet kitten.'

Time lost all meaning that night as they strayed back into the raging passion of the past, both taking and receiving until they were fully sated, enfolded together in tired warmth, their bodies entwined in intimate rest as they drifted into sleep.

It was early morning when Leigh awoke and she remembered instantly where she was, turning to find Raoul fast asleep stretched out beside her, his long, thick lashes resting on the high cheekbones below which dark stubble was beginning to show.

She lay for a long time just looking at him, feasting her eyes on every line and contour of his face as she relived their conversation in minute detail.

Did she believe him? She let her eyes wander over the lean muscled body only partially concealed beneath the sheet. Yes, she believed him. When she was here with him like this. When he could reach out and touch her and make her believe that black was white. But that wasn't good enough to build the rest of their lives on. She had to be sure, totally sure, and she needed to be alone to think, without his sensual presence to detract and confuse.

She slid out of bed carefully, padding into her room on silent feet and dressing quickly in jeans and a warm jumper. She would go for a walk in the early morning air to clear her head.

She could hear Colette in the kitchen as she quietly left after stopping to fuss Oscar, who had returned after his night on the tiles, just outside the front door but didn't call to explain her whereabouts. She didn't want to speak to anyone just at the moment.

She found her mind was remarkably clear as she walked through the grounds in the warm morning air fresh with the scent of a hundred flowers beneath a sky washed clean and a brilliant blue. Her decision was made. The thought was no surprise. It had been made the moment he had explained the circumstances surrounding Marion. She had just needed time to adjust, to allow herself to feel again, to take in the enormity of trusting him completely. It was frightening and intimidating but breathtakingly intoxicating.

She loved him. She hugged the reality she had tried to smother for so long to her tightly like a mother with a newborn baby. She could believe again, live again, look forward to a future enriched with his presence, maybe children...grandchildren.

She believed him when he said there had never been anyone else but her. Not all men were like her father and Raoul was not responsible for his devastating good looks. A conversation they had had in the early days of their marriage came back to her with stark clarity. She had just told him she loved him, which had not been unusual, but he had taken hold of her hand and kissed it as he had muttered thank you against her mouth.

'Thank you?' She remembered she had laughed, thinking he was joking. 'What are you thanking me for?'

'For loving the real me,' he had said slowly. 'You are the first woman I've met who has wanted to get beyond my looks and my wealth. If I were penniless tomorrow or injured and disfigured you'd still love me, wouldn't you, Leigh?'

'Of course.' She had stared at him in amazement. 'You know that.'

'Yes, I do.' He had smothered her with kisses then. 'I just can't believe you're real at times, and I certainly don't deserve you.'

Oh, Raoul... The glorious conviction that she was doing the right thing was cemented into place. She would never doubt him again; she would never have to.

As she walked back to the house the sun had risen to its full height, a big burning ball in the clear blue sky. She found herself humming in time to the singing of her heart. After all the desolation, all the tears, all the lonely days and even lonelier nights they had found each other again. It had all been a mistake, a terrible mistake, but they could take back the years that the locust had eaten. They had the rest of their lives after all.

Oscar was sunning himself on a low wall as she neared the house and she stopped for a minute to stroke the soft, silky fur, the sound of his purring like an express train. 'Are you hungry, baby?' she asked him quietly. 'Let's go and get you some food, then.'

As they walked up the walkway and into the back of the hall she met Suzanne at the entrance to the kitchen. '*Madame*?' She missed the note of apprehension in the girl's voice although later it came back to her.

'Oscar's hungry, Suzanne.' She smiled happily. 'Is my husband down yet?'

'Yes—no—I mean...' As Suzanne's voice faltered to a halt she heard Raoul's voice, low and deep, from the study a few feet away, and then the sound of a husky, gurgly female laugh.

'Suzanne?' She stared into the maid's face as her blood froze to ice. No. It couldn't be. It just couldn't. Lots of women laughed like that. 'Who is that with Mr de Chevnair?'

'*Madame*.' Suzanne took a step towards her with her plump arms outstretched and then stopped abruptly, her round face flushing. '*Madame* ...'

'It's all right, Suzanne.' She was going to get no help from the maid; the girl seemed transfixed. Leigh forced her feet to walk along the hall, moving silently on the thick lush carpet with Oscar at her heels until she came to the study.

The door was open the merest crack but the merest crack was all she needed to witness the destruction of her life for the second time. Raoul was standing looking down at Marion, who was standing just in front of him, and his dark face was warm and his eyes gentle.

As she watched, horror-stricken and utterly unable to move, Marion reached up on tiptoe and kissed him, her slim perfect body seductively inviting and her blonde hair shimmering in the bright morning sunlight. They looked magnificent together, two perfect specimens of the human race, and for a moment Leigh really thought she had stopped breathing because of the incredibly sharp pain that pierced her heart.

How she backed away she didn't know; her legs were trembling so much that she would have sworn they were incapable of supporting her, but then she had passed Suzanne, still standing in silence at the far end of the hall, and was out in the fresh morning air, picking up her handbag automatically from where she had placed it on a chair the night before when she had returned home with Raoul, along with the car keys he had slung by its side as he had gathered her up into his arms before carrying her up the stairs.

Oscar followed her out of the front door and without thinking she lifted the cat's warm fluffy body into her arms, settling him on the back seat before starting the engine and driving out of Raoul's life.

CHAPTER TEN

'LOUISA? You are unwell?' As Leigh left the tiny bathroom at the back of the house for the third time in fifteen minutes, she met Michelle standing in the hall outside, obviously waiting for her, plump arms folded over her ample bosom.

'Not really.' She smiled shakily. 'It's just this slight nausea over the last few weeks—it's worse today. It's strange, I've normally got a strong stomach but...' She shrugged slowly.

The old woman eyed her impassively and then took her arm firmly, leading her back up the stairs to the small bedroom she occupied with Oscar and which doubled as a studio. 'Sit down, Louisa.' She pushed her gently on to the bed, casting a quick scathing glance at Oscar stretched out on the covers—he took the hint and skulked off to his basket in the corner.

'I want you to listen to me for a minute, little one.' The old woman sat down beside her, the faint smell of fish that permeated the house more redolent with her closeness. Leigh took a deep breath and prayed for control. She couldn't be sick again. Not now. 'You told us when you arrived here that your husband had died recently?' Leigh nodded warily. 'And you needed a break, to get away?' Leigh nodded again. 'How long...?' The old woman paused, considering her words. 'How long since you were left alone?'

'How long?' Leigh stared at Michelle in consternation. When she had arrived in the little fishing village that awful night six weeks ago she had been barely coherent. She had intended to go inland but had lost her way in the dark, unable to concentrate on anything but the image of Raoul and Marion printed on the screen of her mind. It had been foolish to drive in such a condition, she recognised that, but she hadn't cared at that moment whether she lived or died. It was only Oscar, purring gently on the back seat, who had prompted her to seek an overnight bed in the small village she had chanced on. She couldn't risk hurting him.

'Not long . . . a few weeks.' She stared wide-eyed at the small woman whose dour face hid a heart of gold. Michelle had been sitting with her husband, Henri, and some other locals in the village square enjoying a last glass of wine before they went their separate ways when she had drawn to a halt by their sides, asking if they knew of a bed for the night.

The men had shook their grey heads, mumbling to themselves at the waywardness of the younger generation. 'Not at this time of night,' one of them had said reprovingly, but Michelle had absorbed the white face and huge empty eyes and had risen immediately, hauling her husband to his feet.

'We have a spare room,' she had said slowly. 'One night is no trouble and it is late.'

One night had stretched into many more and the old couple had been content with her explanation of her husband's untimely death and the need to

distance herself for a time from all that was familiar. Michelle had been less than enchanted with
Oscar, who was delighted to be in the house of a
fisherman, stealing the odd morsel whenever he
could and generally creating consternation wherever
he went. Leigh had felt in a kind of limbo, not
daring to think or feel or plan, living each day as
it came and sleeping most nights with Oscar curled
into the small of her back as she lay in a semi-doze
of vivid dreams and swirling nightmares. The cat
seemed quite content with his new surroundings,
highly gratified to have his beloved mistress all to
himself. And he had kept her sane. She blessed the
impulse that had made her bring him with her. He
was not the kind of animal to be ignored and each
time, in the first few days, that she had sunk into
the helpless lethargy that was threatening to take
her over, he had pulled her back with his demands
for food and love, normally in that order.

'Louisa? Listen to me.' Michelle had taken hold
of her hands now and was kneeling in front of her,
her lined face deeply concerned. 'Are you expecting a baby?'

'A baby?' Leigh stared at the old woman
vacantly. She had given a false name on her arrival,
Louisa Chambers, and after her meagre supply of
money had run out she had started to paint in order to pay her way and had been amazed at the
demand for her sketches and paintings from the
tourists who visited the small fishing town,
somehow settling into a niche that was not of her
own making. A baby?

'Michelle...' As she breathed the old woman's
name Michelle saw the realisation dawn in the liquid

brown eyes in front of her and nodded her wise old head slowly.

'Your husband has not left you, little one,' she said softly. 'You will have his child to comfort your days.'

'It can't be!' As her mind winged back she thought about the last two months and how she had put the non-appearance of her normal cycle first down to the tension and excitement of being with Raoul again and then to the shock of seeing him with Marion. But a baby? She thought quickly. It must have been that first time, in the little dell surrounded by trees. That would make her almost three months pregnant.

'You are pleased, Louisa?' She became aware that Michelle was watching her closely, her lined old face creased with concern, and suddenly in that instant she needed to tell this new friend the truth.

When she had finished Michelle was quite silent for a long time and then she resumed her seat on the bed by Leigh, her rheumy eyes clouded with worry. 'This man, your husband, he needs to be told, you know this?'

'No, Michelle!' Leigh's voice was like a pistol shot and the plump body next to hers jumped violently. 'Please, I mean it. If I can't have your promise that you will keep quiet about all this then I'll go now, this minute. Maybe I should anyway. I've imposed long enough as it is.'

'Leigh, Leigh . . .' Michelle took her hands soothingly. 'You have my word, little one, but you will stay here for the moment. You are in no state to go anywhere. Later we will think again and decide

what is best. You must see a doctor, you understand this?' Leigh nodded slowly. 'And you must
try to eat, child. You are so thin.'

'Thin?' Again her physical condition had not entered Leigh's mind for weeks, but now as she
glanced at the full-length mirror on the front of the
small wardrobe in her room she realised just how
slender she had become. She hadn't felt like eating
in the last few weeks, assuming the feeling of nausea
that had intensified with each passing day was
caused by stress rather than anything physical. Her
face looked quite thin, she thought interestedly. It
was the first time she had seen it like that! A baby!
As the idea took shape a deep thrill replaced the
shock and surprise. Raoul's child. Her hand flitted
instinctively to the small mound already visible
under the loose cotton dress she was wearing. She
should have known but she hadn't wanted to think,
to observe, anything.

It would never have a father. As Michelle left
and she settled back on the bed, Oscar immediately
joining her to settle in a warm, comfortable heap
at her side, the thought leapt out at her condemn-
ingly. But it would have a mother who would love
it enough for both, she argued mentally. Her marriage to Raoul was finished, totally and irrevo-
cably, but now as she allowed the camera in her
mind to dwell on his face she knew she would never
stop loving him. And she would have their child.
Would she tell him? She shook her head against the
thought. Not yet, perhaps not ever. It was enough
for now just to be. She felt as though she had come

through the worst she could ever experience but she *had* come through and now... Now was the first day of the rest of her life.

Three weeks later, due to the nagging of Michelle rather than anything else, she accompanied the old woman to the doctor's in the next town, driving Raoul's car carefully. She hadn't driven it since that fateful day she had left the house, leaving it parked in the old disused garage at the back of Michelle's and Henri's tiny cottage, but there was none of the blinding horror and outrage that had gripped her that day. There was a searing ache in her heart whenever she thought of Raoul but the wonder of the new life growing inside her was beginning to fill all her thoughts and plans.

When she emerged from the doctor's surgery an hour later and joined Michelle in the Range Rover the Frenchwoman glanced anxiously at her pale face. 'What is it, Leigh?' The old woman reached out and rubbed Leigh's hands between her own. 'What is wrong?'

'He thinks it's twins.' Leigh's voice was faint with shock. 'If I've got my dates right, and there can be no question about that, then I've either got a baby elephant in there or twins.' She glanced down at the quite distinct mound made even more prominent by her loss of weight everywhere else.

'Leigh, you must tell your husband.' Michelle's voice was full of anxiety. 'If nothing else he must find you a place to live and have your babies, provide money for their upkeep and——'

'Don't, Michelle.' Leigh leaned wearily against the seat warmed by the autumn sunshine, the summer having departed, and shut her eyes for a moment. 'It'll all work out; just give me some time.'

'I'm worried about you.' Leigh opened her eyes and looked into the face of the woman who had become like a mother to her in the short time she had known her. 'How will you manage?'

'Far better than if I see Raoul again,' Leigh said softly, an aching sadness turning her eyes black. 'Please, Michelle, no more.'

The ride home was conducted in silence and Leigh disappeared to her room as soon as she could to a rapturous welcome from Oscar. She spent the rest of the day painting from some sketches she had taken weeks before of the quaint little waterfront, the fishing boats tethered in the foreground and the wide expanse of the sea beyond.

As the violet mist of dusk dulled the light she decided to have a bath, always an exhausting procedure in the tiny little bathroom where the water was supplied by an ageing boiler that croaked and groaned and laboured to fill the small bath.

The day had been a warm one, a last fling of late summer before the chilly fingers of autumn really took hold, and on re-entering her room she pulled on the old cotton nightie Michelle had lent her weeks before, its limited fullness already pulling tight over the raised mound of her stomach. She patted the bump, as she had seen countless pregnant women do in the past, and smiled softly to herself. Who would have thought it? After plaiting her hair behind her head, leaving her neck free to the slight breeze that was blowing in through the open window, she fed Oscar the fish Michelle had saved him from their lunch and went to sit in the old battered chair by the window as the sky turned pewter-dark and filled the small room with black shadows.

Over the last few weeks she had trained her mind not to think of Raoul, it was the only way to get by, but now, annoyingly, her imagination was hearing his voice and the illusion sent shivers trembling down her spine. She brushed her hand across her eyes angrily. Stop it right now, she cautioned herself sternly. None of that.

As the door opened without even a preliminary knock and she turned she was concious of two things registering simultaneously on her stunned senses. Raoul, huge and dark and angry in the doorway, and Michelle behind him, a small squat figure incongruous against the lean body beside her, her round face stretched tight with apprehension and her arms waving wildly.

'Raoul . . . ?' Her voice was faint but he heard it, his eyes peering through the darkness towards her as she still sat frozen in the chair, Michelle disappearing quickly from view.

'Who else were you expecting?' His voice bit through the air with searing fury. 'I've searched France for you the last two months, woman! What the hell are you playing at? I didn't know if you were alive or dead. When Suzanne said you had just walked out looking as though you were going to faint—hell, Leigh!' He swore softly and fluently in his native tongue. 'How could you leave me like that?'

The light from the landing behind him had illuminated the big figure with an aura of yellow but she was a pale blur in the darkness, and as the buzzing in her ears grew louder she stood up slowly, beyond the ability to think or feel, dumb and shaking.

'Well?' His voice was a snarl as he watched her falter to the middle of the room like a blind woman, her eyes enormous in the stark whiteness of her face. As she reached the shaft of light from the door she saw his eyes widen but by then the rushing express train that was pounding through her head had reached its crescendo and she fell, with a little disbelieving whimper, into a dead faint on the floor, stretched out in front of him like a slender ethereal ghost.

She was struggling to come out of the noisy swirling blackness for some time before she managed to surface and open her heavy eyes. For a moment the image in front of her meant nothing as her senses fought to emerge from the screaming confusion of the subconscious and make sense of the real world, and then as Raoul spoke her name, softly and desperately, she focused on him and realised she was lying on the bed with her hands in his as he knelt by her side.

'Leigh?' She had never seen him look like this in all the time she had known him. 'Leigh, can you hear me? Say something.' His hands were shaking so badly that she could feel the tremors in her own body and the burning anguish in his eyes reached out to her, forcing her to speak.

'Raoul?' She tried to move but it was as though dead weights were fixed to her limbs. 'How...?'

'Michelle.' He answered the question she hadn't asked as with a harsh cry of relief he gathered her up into his arms, sitting on the bed as he eased her on to his lap, pulling the quilted cover round her trembling body. He rocked back and forwards for a few seconds in an agony of thankfulness and although her mind was burning with questions she couldn't speak through the immense tiredness that seemed to have taken her over. 'How could you go like that?' he asked again against the silk of her hair. 'You've nearly sent me insane.'

'How could I...?' Now fierce anger gave her the burst of adrenalin she needed to struggle against the arms holding her so close.

'Don't, please.' As he moved his head to stare into her face the look in his eyes took all her strength. She had never thought to see such naked misery on the face of any human being, let alone Raoul, and it cut through her bitter pain like an electric shock. 'Michelle contacted me tonight, through the car, the registration number; the police have been looking for it for weeks. She told me you were here but I didn't know...' His voice trailed away as his hand moved to the mound of her stomach, hesitating just above her body before falling back to his side. 'When Suzanne saw you take Oscar I assumed you hadn't left France because of him; I knew you wouldn't risk quarantine.'

'And Marion?' She had the most uncomfortable feeling, now the first shock of his presence had receded, that she was going to be sick. Not now, in front of him, she prayed silently. She hadn't had the nausea for days; please not now.

'You saw me with Marion? I assumed when Suzanne said you had left like that——'

'Please, Raoul, I have to go to the bathroom...' She had stumbled off his lap and was out of the door before he could move, but as she fled down the stairs and into the tiny room at the back of the house she was mortified to hear he was following her—but then the retching took all her attention, leaving her trembling and giddy. As she went to slump on the floor at last, totally spent, he gathered her up in his arms with a smothered oath, carrying her back to her room as he yelled for Michelle at the top of his voice.

'Is it supposed to be like this?' As the small woman joined them in the bedroom, he laid Leigh tenderly on the covers before turning to Michelle, his eyes sharp with concern. 'She's lost pounds in weight. Is everything normal?'

'More than normal,' Leigh said weakly from the bed. 'Do twins run in your family, by any chance?'

'Twins?' The result of her bombshell was more satisfying than the two times she had hit him, Leigh reflected wryly to herself as she watched his eyes widen in incredulous disbelief, his eyes flying to her swollen stomach with a mixture of fear and wonder on his face before returning to her pale face. 'Twins?' She had never thought to see him completely out of his depth but she was seeing it now. He stared at her as though she was the most amazing thing he had ever seen. 'Are you sure?'

'More or less.' She tried for casualness but her voice was shaking so much the effect was spoilt. 'Either that or——'

'Or what?' he cut in sharply.

'Three or four.'

'Don't joke,' he said weakly. As Michelle disappeared again, her eyes anxious, Raoul closed the door behind her and walked over to kneel by the bed. 'Listen to me,' he said urgently. 'When you saw me with Marion——' She raised her hand to protest but he put one hand over her mouth as he caught her wrist with the other. 'When you saw me with Marion she had come to see *you*, to explain.'

'Explain?' Her voice was muffled in the palm of his hand but he heard her anyway.

'I hadn't seen her or Paul since that night I drove them to the airport but apparently they brought a house in La Rochelle in the end. Marion heard through a mutual friend that you had come back and she wanted to apologise to us both but especially you, to tell you that what she had felt for me was infatuation and that she loves Paul. He stood by her, you know, even when she told him the truth. A "summer madness" was how she described it.' He looked at her warily, his eyes roaming over her face with a hunger in their depths that he couldn't quite hide. 'She wanted to tell you the truth herself, I think she's been racked with guilt for years that she broke our marriage.'

'Good,' said Leigh guardedly. She dared not believe this. She just dared not.

'When did you see us?' he asked painfully.

'Just as she kissed you.' Leigh kept her eyes tight on his face, watching his every expression.

'It was a kiss from a friend, a gesture, a thank-you that I had consented to see her,' Raoul said quietly. 'She had thought she would be turned away at the door.'

Leigh stared at him silently as her heart started to pound. Not again. She couldn't go through it all again.

'I love you, Leigh, no one on earth exists for me except you, I don't give that much——' he flicked his fingers sharply '—for anyone else, *anyone else*. I can't explain adequately how I feel, I don't think I ever will be able to, but without you there is nothing. The only thing that kept me going through the last few years was your image carved in my mind and in my garden.' He laughed shakily. 'I spent hours looking at that damn piece of marble.'

'What?' She stared at him in bewilderment.

'The statue. You must have realised——' He stopped abruptly at her bewildered face. 'The statue; you didn't know it was you?'

'Me?' She sat up slowly. The statue, the breathtakingly lovely statue, rising like a phoenix from the ashes in the place where she had burnt all her ties with this man. 'But it's beautiful...'

'It can't compare with the real thing,' he said huskily.

'I'm not beautiful, Raoul,' she said, flatly refusing to acknowledge this thing that was threatening to burst forth into glorious life deep inside her. 'I wasn't before, but now...' She gestured towards her stomach and with a smothered groan he placed his hand on the mound below which his children's hearts were beating.

He didn't speak but as the tears ran down his cheeks his eyes said it all and in that second she understood. He was hers, totally, completely and for eternity. He always had been. As she fell against him, her arms going round his neck as he pulled her close, all the doubts, all the fears of the past were consumed.

'Love me,' she whispered against the wetness of his cheek as she took his face in her hands, finding his mouth with a hunger that matched his. 'Now.'

'But the babies…' He indicated her stomach with a flick of his hand even as she felt his body stir against hers through the thin cotton of her nightie.

'They're going to have to get used to having a mum and dad who are hopelessly in love,' she murmured softly, 'so they might as well adapt from the start.'

And so it was.

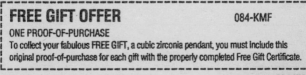

Take 4 bestselling love stories FREE

Plus get a FREE surprise gift!

Special Limited-time Offer

Mail to Harlequin Reader Service®

3010 Walden Avenue
P.O. Box 1867
Buffalo, N.Y. 14240-1867

YES! Please send me 4 free Harlequin Presents® novels and my free surprise gift. Then send me 6 brand-new novels every month, which I will receive months before they appear in bookstores. Bill me at the low price of $2.90 each plus 25¢ delivery and applicable sales tax, if any*. That's the complete price and a savings of over 10% off the cover prices—quite a bargain! I understand that accepting the books and gift places me under no obligation ever to buy any books. I can always return a shipment and cancel at any time. Even if I never buy another book from Harlequin, the 4 free books and the surprise gift are mine to keep forever.

106 BPA A3UL

Name	(PLEASE PRINT)	
Address		Apt. No.
City	State	Zip

This offer is limited to one order per household and not valid to present Harlequin Presents® subscribers. *Terms and prices are subject to change without notice. Sales tax applicable in N.Y.

UPRES-696   ©1990 Harlequin Enterprises Limited

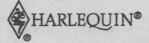